The Observer's Pocket Series

FIREARMS

Observer's Books

The Observer's Book of
FIREARMS

NICHOLAS DU QUESNE BIRD

WITH 119 BLACK AND WHITE PHOTOGRAPHS
AND 9 LINE DRAWINGS

FREDERICK WARNE
LONDON

First published 1978 by
Frederick Warne (Publishers) Ltd,
London

ISBN 0 7232 1571 5

Filmset and reproduced by BAS Printers Limited,
Over Wallop, Hampshire and printed in Great Britain by
William Clowes Ltd, London, Beccles and Colchester
2701-278

CONTENTS

ACKNOWLEDGEMENTS

I should like to express my gratitude to the staff of the Pattern Room, Army Quality Assurance Directorates, Enfield Lock, and to Major F. Myatt M.C. and Mr Davie of the School of Infantry, Warminster. Without their generous help many of the more interesting and unusual firearms could not have been illustrated, and this book could not have appeared in its present form.

The line drawings were by Ray Martin.

The photographers were Richard Traube, Brian Gentry Long, and the author. Photographs were also supplied by the School of Infantry, the Sterling Armament Co. Ltd., the Solartron Electronic Group Ltd., the National History Museum, Stockholm, and the Tøjhusmuseet, Copenhagen.

The arms illustrated are from the following sources, the numbers indicating the pages upon which the illustrations occur. The sources are also indicated by initials at the end of the description of each firearm.

City Museum, Bristol: 68, 70, 71, 92–94, 105, 119, 120, 128, 181

Moxham's Antiques, Bradford-on-Avon: 95

National History Museum, Stockholm: 56, 57

Pattern Room, Army Quality Assurance Directorates (W), Enfield Lock: 62, 74, 80, 85, 97–100, 103, 106, 108, 110, 112, 121–7, 129, 132–9, 141, 142, 144–53, 155–61, 163–73, 175–9, 183, 184

Quinney's Antiques, Bristol: 69, 72, 91, 96, 101, 182

School of Infantry, Warminster: 59, 73, 75–9, 81–4, 86, 87, 104, 107, 109, 111, 130

Solartron Electronic Group Ltd: 185

Sterling Armament Company Ltd: 174

Tøjhusmuseet, Copenhagen: 58

INTRODUCTION

It is difficult, often impossible, for the collector of antique firearms, or the shooting man, to explain his enthusiasm to another person. All collectors and enthusiasts, whatever the subject of their interest, have this difficulty to some degree.

Firearms are lethal weapons intended to kill men and animals, and it may be suggested that the only reason for an interest in them is a morbid interest in violence. This charge has no foundation when levelled against the true enthusiast.

The target shot knows the difficulty of obtaining a high score, and takes his pleasure in this. He shoots without considering that the bullseye once represented the vital parts of an enemy. His is a strict and exacting sport, in which many countries have teams competing at an international level. The hunter and the wild-fowler take a pride in their knowledge of their game and its conservation, and they know the difficulty of the hunt, and the pleasure of returning home, perhaps weary and dirty, but with a full bag. The collector comes to realize that each gun has an intrinsic fascination, perhaps a beauty, of its own. The purpose for which a weapon was intended may seldom enter his mind, indeed, many collectors never fire a shot. Not to think of the gun as having been intended as a lethal weapon is not the conscious repression of an unpleasant fact, but simply an awareness that a gun may have a mechanical or aesthetic appeal quite unrelated to its lethal purpose.

Behind the modern gun lies some six hundred years of development. Until the last century, each gun was made by a craftsman, or a small team of craftsmen. Until mechanization, most guns were unique: the perfectly matched pair is a rarity. All forms of decoration have been used, from the simple treatment of metals and woods to reveal their structure, to the use of precious metals and gems. Fine engraving, inlay, and precious metals are still features of many modern guns.

A simple and well-designed mechanism, whatever its purpose, has a beauty of its own. It is no less to be appreciated when designed and built in a factory. The modern weapons designer is no less a craftsman than his forbears.

The collection and study of antique firearms, by large numbers of people, is a relatively young pursuit. It is a specialized branch of the collection and study of antique weapons in general, which became popular during the nineteenth century, as did most antiquarian interests. Interest in firearms, and arms and armour in general, has increased enormously during the last thirty years. This interest has continued to increase, and the demand for antique arms causes their price to rise continually. Only the very wealthiest collector can hope to obtain the finest and earliest pieces, but the collector of modest means can still build up an important collection of guns which are still moderately priced. A carefully built up collection can provide not only many hours of pleasure, but a valuable investment as prices continue to rise.

As in any other field of interest, the observant and knowledgeable collector does stand some chance of making a fabulous find. The unrecognized and important pieces have to be found somewhere.

All possible avenues of research have not yet been completed. There are a number of virtually unexplored by-ways open to new collectors. As the number of collectors grows, the number of specialized branches of arms collecting increases. The individual collector has a correspondingly increased ability, by his own industry, to increase the sum of our knowledge of antique arms.

In this book an attempt has been made to show the development of the gun from the most primitive hand-held cannon to the most sophisticated assault rifle. The collector cannot normally acquire weapons at either end of this spectrum, but to see his collection in context, some study of the whole picture is needed.

The Collection

An interest in antique firearms usually has a basis in handling some firearm or other. The sporting shot or the serviceman may discover in himself an interest in the development and ancestry of the firearms which he uses. Or interest may derive from the chance discovery of some long forgotten sporting gun, pistol, or war trophy.

In the beginning the collector does not specialize. His interest is in firearms as a whole, and he may buy anything and everything that he can afford to buy and can legally possess. Some collectors, particularly those who use their guns, never do specialize, but will buy anything that works and is safe to use, from matchlock guns to semi-automatic rifles, simple because an interest is taken in the different classes of mechanism and in the different skills required to use these guns.

It is inevitable that some of the purchases made in the first flush of enthusiasm will be regretted later, but they should not be regretted too strongly. Without these initial purchases the collector may find it difficult to establish in which precise class of weapons he is most interested. Every firearm, of any class, adds something to the collector's experience and knowledge of arms as a whole, and it is that experience and knowledge which he most lacks at the beginning. Unless the initial purchases were extremely unwise, a stock is built up

9

which may be exchanged or sold at a later date, perhaps profitably.

A general approach may be followed for some time, until more interest is taken in one particular class of weapons than in others. A type of mechanism, such as the flintlock, may evoke some response, and a collection of English flintlock pistols may be formed. A geographical approach may be adopted, and the collector may seek guns made in the area where he lives. An interest in military history may lead the collector to specialize in weapons used in a particular war, or by a particular army or regiment. The possible approaches are numerous.

In these days of small houses it is often the case that collections are limited in some directions, in accordance with what can reasonably be stored. The collector may be able to think of nothing nicer than to live in a house which resembles an arsenal, but the other members of his family may not see this in the same light. For reasons such as this, pistols can be significantly more expensive than muskets and rifles. There is a great demand for them, because they are more easily stored and displayed.

In the beginning the collector will lack experience. It is important that as many weapons are handled as possible. Only by handling a variety of weapons can the collector learn what is commonplace and what is not, and what is genuine and what is not. Museums and art galleries should be visited, not only to see those weapons which are displayed, but those which are not. Most museums will have some weapons in reserve collections, which the curator will allow to be examined and handled. The weapons held in reserve may be less important than those on display, but may be of more use to the student as they can be examined more closely and handled. Specialist dealers and gunsmiths may allow enthusiasts to handle their stock, but they do not have an unlimited amount of time and patience. Other collectors should be approached: the majority of collectors are delighted to show their acquisitions to fellow enthusiasts. A particularly useful time and place for examining a wide variety of firearms is on the viewing day of an arms auction. An auction catalogue is purchased, and there may be sufficient time to examine each piece closely.

Another type of experience is to see guns in use, or to use them. Without taking any particular interest in shooting, the enthusiast may well be interested in the performance and capabilities of one of the guns he has. This is not to suggest that he fire it. The particular gun of interest may well be very unsafe to fire, and the collector may not be legally authorized to fire it or any other gun. However, there are a number of clubs whose members fire either antique guns or replicas of them. A visit to the ranges when such guns are being fired, and talking to the people who fire them, may be an interesting and useful experience. The local gunsmith will often know where and when such shooting is being done. It may also be interesting to try to shoot with some modern guns. In most areas there are clubs, which the local gunsmith will know about. Many clubs have club guns. Upon payment of a small fee, usually for range maintenance and insurance, and the cost of the ammunition, the enthusiast can spend an interesting evening, or a few hours at a weekend, shooting with one of the club guns. If a sporting gun is added to the collection, some idea of the use and handling of sporting guns may be gathered from following a pheasant shoot, or a deer hunt, or accompanying some wildfowlers. The designs of many target weapons and sporting guns have hardly changed in the last century, so the experience of handling them or seeing them in use may be more relevant that it seems.

Until the collector is competent to judge the material

11

he is being offered, guns should only be bought from specialist dealers, from specialist auctioneers, and from reputable antique dealers. These people have their reputations to protect, and that is the collector's safeguard. They will not knowingly sell a gun without pointing out any dubious features it may have, and may provide a receipt describing the gun sold exactly. Some dealers will allow goods to be taken on approval, by collectors known to them, but since it is open to abuse, this custom is rare. Dealers may buy back goods which prove not to be what they purported to be, and some dealers will allow goods to be returned within a specified period of time if they are found unsatisfactory for any reason. Specialist auctioneers have clear descriptions of the weapon being sold printed in their auction catalogues, and their reputation depends on the accuracy of these descriptions. They are confident of their expertise, and careful of their reputations, and for these reasons will not always admit legal responsibility for the accuracy of their descriptions or for faults in any lot. In theory, the prospective buyer has had ample time to examine guns which he may wish to purchase.

Ill-judged buying from non-specialist dealers not only permits the dealer's mistakes to be passed on to his customers, but can result in higher prices being paid. The general dealer may have no particular knowledge of firearms, but he has trade periodicals and auction catalogues, and it is often upon these that he bases his prices. A common gun may be very similar indeed to a rare one. The dealer may base his price solely upon the photograph of a gun, and a record of how much was paid for it at auction. He may honestly believe that his gun ought to fetch as much, and he may be quite right or quite wrong. It can certainly be worthwhile to visit antique dealers in the search for guns, but to make it really worthwhile the collector must be more knowledgeable in his chosen field than the antique dealer. This is not very difficult, as the antique dealer not only has his own speciality, but has to have some knowledge of a very wide variety of other antiques. It is still possible to buy rare firearms from antique dealers at moderate prices, but at the same time many antique dealers are tending to overprice the commonplace pieces, to avoid making mistakes, and to leave themselves more room in which to haggle with the more specialized dealers whom they may be supplying.

Antique markets and street markets can be most useful sources for unusual material. Rare pieces can turn up in such places before they reach the antique shops or specialist dealers. The collector competes with the antique dealers who are circulating in their never-ending search for stock, and must arrive as early as possible, as anything of interest will change hands and increase in price amongst the stall-holders as soon as it is spotted by them. It must be realized that the market may be the first choice of the person who wishes to dispose of bad pieces, forgeries and stolen goods, as there is no other place where he may find so many ill-informed dealers in so short a time.

Buying from general auctioneers can be rewarding, but can also be hazardous for the unwary. The catalogue description is of necessity brief, and may give a false impression. The auctioneers have no great knowledge of firearms, and the collector may have to bid against antique dealers who may also have no great knowledge of firearms. The auctioneer will sell the lots as they stand, and there may be no recourse if the pieces are not genuine, unless they are stated to be genuine in the catalogue.

When buying from auctioneers, whether they are specialist or not, it is of the greatest importance to examine the lots carefully beforehand, and to read the conditions of sale at the beginning of the auction catalogue. The collector should remember that the forger may conveniently disperse his products through auction rooms, and that antique dealers' mistakes are often disposed of through the auction room. It is a sensible practice to visit the auction room on several occasions before buying, to compare the lots with the catalogue, so that it can be judged how much reliance may be placed upon it in the future, and to see how the sale is carried out. No reputable auctioneer will knowingly publish a false or misleading description, but a general auctioneer has to handle a wide variety of goods, and cannot be expected to be well-informed about all of them.

If personal attendance at an auction is impossible it is often possible to submit a postal bid. If the bid is successful, the gun is held for collection, but charges may be levied for storage and insurance. If it is possible, it is better for the inexperienced collector to use a commission buyer. He will charge a percentage, but may advise the collector as to what price would be reasonable, and will not bid if he has any reservations about the authenticity of the piece, unless he is instructed to. Alternatively, a dealer known to the collector may bid for him.

Few people can afford to build up a collection of firearms without ever selling any. The collector may have to sell some pieces in order to be able to afford others, or may simply wish to dispose of a particular specimen when he has a better example.

Usually the best way to dispose of unwanted guns is to sell them to another collector, or to sell them in part-exchange for a gun that is wanted. However, it may not be possible to do this at the right time. The easiest way to sell is to an arms dealer or an antique dealer. It is in the dealer's interest to be available all the time, and to buy any weapon in reasonable condition. But unless some time has passed since the gun was bought, the collector cannot expect to get his money back or make a profit. The dealer has to make his living.

A further means of disposal is the specialist auctioneer. If ready money is needed, this is the slowest method. A detailed description must be provided for the auctioneer, who may nevertheless choose to write his own description, and who may sell the gun as part of a lot rather than a lot in itself. A reserve price has to be given: this is the lowest price at which the gun can be sold. If the gun deserves an illustration in the catalogue, this may have to be paid for. A commission will be charged of between 5 and 15 per cent. An additional charge may be payable if the gun fails to reach reserve. Some auctioneers may allow a cash advance of a certain percentage of their valuation of the goods submitted.

Collectors sometimes have the greatest difficulty in deciding the price they ought to pay for guns, and the value of them when they wish to sell them. The only reliable way of obtaining an idea of current prices is to subscribe to auction catalogues. Either the prices realized will be published in the catalogue following the previous sale, or they will be available from the auctioneer on payment of a fee. Naturally, another gun in exactly the same condition, of exactly the same type and date, and by the same maker will not normally be found in a dozen auction catalogues, but some idea of the price of guns in the same class and condition can be obtained. A specialist auctioneer or a competent dealer may be asked to value a piece, and may charge some percentage of that value or a nominal fee, in addition to expenses. A gun is worth precisely what people are prepared to pay for it. The more people want it, the higher the price it will fetch. When buying in competition with others, the collector should set the price he is prepared to pay beforehand, and not allow himself to be driven above this.

Display and Storage

Glass-fronted cabinets are probably the ideal, but are seldom practical unless the collector has a room which he can use solely for his guns. The majority of collectors can display their pieces against some area of wall. Since from time to time pieces will be added or disposed of, or it may be desirable to alter the display, some flexibility in the method of hanging the pieces is useful. An inexpensive and simple expedient is to use peg-board. This allows a wide variety of metal supports. Sometimes it will be impossible to use any of the supports commercially available, but individual supports can easily be made from stout wire. If the area of peg-board is properly installed, it will support all but the heaviest of guns.

Before constructing a display unit, it is sensible to visit a number of arms dealers and antique dealers to examine their methods of display.

No arms should be hung up where any condensation can take place, as this will quickly ruin them. A simple test is to hang up a length of metal pipe against the wall which it is intended to use. If the pipe becomes moist or rusts, another area should be sought.

If arms are usable or intended to be used, the police may well insist that they, or some component part of them, are kept in a safe, or in a room with a good lock and a secure window. A number of good firearms safes are commercially available, and many are not expensive. A number are advertised which are little more than metal clothes lockers: these should be avoided.

If a collection consists largely of pistols, these can be stored in a filing cabinet with shallow drawers, or in some similar piece of furniture. The drawers can be lined with foam rubber blocks or cuttings, overlaid with a coloured fabric. In this way little floor-space is used, a reasonable level of security maintained, and an attractive display unit made.

Arms should never be put away loose, as they can easily be damaged by hitting against each other when drawers are opened or furniture moved. Weapons stored should be wrapped in soft cloths or tissue paper. Cloth may be sprayed with a patent rust inhibitor: the local gunsmith or museum may have their favourites that they can recommend.

Weapons on display will often need regular dusting and oiling, unless they are in glass cabinets.

Insurance and Security

A collection of firearms constantly increases in value, and ought to be revalued annually. Most insurance companies will arrange coverage, but will generally require an independent valuation. This can be done best by a specialist auctioneer, an antique dealer specializing in firearms, or a gunsmith with a knowledge of antique firearms.

In case of loss by theft, it will considerably assist the police if a proper record is kept of each gun. Each one should be photographed, with a tape measure alongside it. Additional close-up photographs should be taken of the actions or locks of long-arms, as these form a relatively small proportion of the photograph of the whole gun, and may not be very clear on the full length photograph. Details peculiar to individual guns, such as engraved shields with crests or initials, or arsenal marks on the butts of rifles, also merit separate photographs. The cost of such photography is small. The photographs do not have to be printed; the negatives can be kept on file. All makers' marks, proof marks and serial numbers should be recorded, as should the calibre of the gun. If the gun is covered by a Firearm Certificate, the maker's name, the serial number and the calibre will be recorded on the certificate.

Following a request at the local police station, the

house where the collection is to be kept can be visited and surveyed by a Crime Prevention Officer. He will submit a written report describing what security measures would be most efficient and practical, and also a list of local locksmiths competent to carry these out. This service is free. When the recommended work has been done, the insurance company should be given the Crime Prevention Officer's report. This, and a proper record of the contents of a collection, may well influence the insurance costs.

The Collector's Will

The formation of a collection is generally of interest only to one member of a family, the collector himself. Relatives and dependants may not have any real idea of the value of it, how and where it was obtained, or how much it cost to build up. They may have even less idea of how to dispose of it. It is therefore essential that the collector stipulates in his will that a specific executor must dispose of the collection. This executor should be a specialist auctioneer or gunsmith. When the collection contains weapons covered by Firearm Certificate or by Shotgun Certificate, the police will normally grant the beneficiary of a will a permit to hold the firearms and ammunition involved until they are disposed of. A specific period of time will probably be stipulated, but if a proper executor has been appointed, this should pose no problem. A solicitor or a banker will be able to offer advice about how this portion of a will should be worded. The bank manager might be the best person to approach, as he may have a good idea of how much money has been spent, and might not charge for his advice.

Firearms and the Law

Unlike other collectors, the collector of firearms may have to contend with a variety of legislation.

Historically, laws relating to arms were enacted to ensure that the people were armed, so that they could keep the peace, and defend their liberty and their country should the need arise. Such laws are still enforced in the more internally stable countries of Western Europe.

During the nineteenth century many national police forces were established, and the need for people to be armed to keep the peace and defend their lives and property theoretically decreased. In many countries laws were enacted to control the carrying of arms, but not their possession.

The early years of the present century saw a small body of legislation designed to ensure that pistols were not sold to children and drunk people. Since the First World War there has been a steady increase in legislation which restricts the possession of firearms. Theoretically these laws decrease the availability of firearms to criminals, and ensure that no body of citizens can take up arms against the state. In practice neither the criminal nor the terrorist pay very much attention to this legislation, and may be neither more nor less likely to use firearms than they were before such legislation was enacted. Naturally, the restrictions fall largely on the legitimate owners and users of firearms, and upon the police who enforce them.

The current British legislation is not unduly restrictive, but it is so constructed as to be capable of being very restrictive in its interpretation. The degrees of restriction may not be established by the democratic decisions of Parliament, but by the purely executive decisions of the Home Office.

In theory, an antique firearm is exempt from the provisions of the current *Firearms Act*, but in practice there is no legal definition of an antique firearm. Different police forces may interpret the law differently. Their interpretation will vary in stringency depending on the attitude towards firearms of senior police officers in different areas, and in accordance with instructions which they may from time to time receive from the Home Office.

A gun purchased as an antique in one area, legitimately and from a respectable dealer, may in another area, or by another police force, be deemed a firearm subject to the act. Under these circumstances, the collector may at best have the gun confiscated or be obliged to dispose of it, at worst he may be imprisoned and fined.

The observations which follow are intended simply for the collector's guidance. It is imperative that the advice of the local police Firearms Officer be sought, and that of the nearest reputable gunsmith. This cannot be emphasized too strongly. The intending collector must find out for himself what he may legally collect, and this will differ from area to area.

(1) *Muzzle-loading weapons, with matchlock, wheel-lock, flintlock or percussion ignition. Breech-loading weapons, with flintlock or percussion ignition, taking a loose charge of powder, or a skin or paper cartridge.*

If genuinely antique, such weapons may generally be held without certificate, provided that they are not fired.

Flintlock and percussion guns are still made, to the original specifications, for use. Unscrupulous individuals have obtained these reproductions, removed the modern proof-marks, and aged them artificially. Such forgeries are subject to the *Firearms Act*, and both the vendor and the purchaser may be prosecuted.

If the gun is to be fired, at least two certificates will be needed. A permit to purchase gunpowder must be obtained from the local Chief Officer of Police. The police will wish to assure themselves that safe provision has been made for the storage of gunpowder.

A fire officer and a crime prevention officer may be called upon to examine this. If permission is granted, the holder is strongly advised to discuss the matter with whichever company is insuring his house. If the barrel of the gun is not rifled, is not less than 24 in. (61 cm) in length, and is intended to be used as a shotgun, then a Shotgun Certificate must be obtained from the local police. If the gun has a rifled barrel, or is a smooth-bore with a barrel less than 24 in. (61 cm) in length, a Firearm Certificate is required. Whether the barrel is rifled or not, and whatever its length, a Firearm Certificate is required if ball rather than shot is to be fired.

If a gun is sold for use, whether antique or reproduction, it must be in proof (see (6) p. 24).

(2) *Early breech-loading weapons taking cartridges containing their own means of ignition.*
Shotguns. A shotgun is defined as a smoothbore weapon having a barrel not less than 24 in. (61 cm) in length. In theory, if such a gun is held as an antique, curiosity or ornament, a Shotgun Certificate is not required.In practice there can be no legal definition of an antique, curiosity, or ornament, and the collector is advised to obtain a Shotgun Certificate from the local police if he wishes to purchase such weapons. A Shotgun Certificate entitles the holder to possess an unspecified number of shotguns.

Ideally the collector should only sell an antique shotgun to a Registered Firearms Dealer or through an auctioneer. If the purchaser should decide to use the gun, and was injured in the resulting explosion, the seller could be prosecuted.

Most police forces express the opinion that any weapon which loads a metallic cartridge from the breech requires a Firearm Certificate. In some areas pinfire weapons are regarded as antique, and in other areas they require a Firearm Certificate. The collector should consult his local police Firearms Officer and his gunsmith.

(3) *Obsolete or obsolescent weapons taking centre-fire cartridges.*

Most police forces require the purchaser to obtain a Firearm Certificate. In some areas very early centre-fire weapons, such as Snider action rifles, may be purchased without certificate. Such guns are regularly advertised. The collector should consult his local police Firearms Officer and his gunsmith.

Many obsolete military rifles become available as the contents of old arsenals are sold. In the majority of cases these are usable weapons for which the ammunition is still available. A Firearm Certificate will be required before these can be purchased.

A number of arms dealers have the rifling bored out of quantities of military rifles, so that they fall within the legal definition of a shotgun. Such smoothbored guns are regularly advertised, and the collector may be able to purchase them if he holds a Shotgun Certificate. Despite the absence of rifling, these guns are capable of firing the ammunition for which they were intended, and some police forces may require a Firearm Certificate to be held in respect of them.

Some early modern military rifles have been converted to .410 calibre or 20 bore shotguns. This does not affect their mechanical operation or their external appearance, and it should be possible for the collector to purchase them if he holds a Shotgun Certificate.

(4) *Prohibited weapons.*

Weapons capable of fully automatic fire, such as machine guns, are generally prohibited, and may only be held on the written authority of the Secretary of State for the Home Office, or the Scottish Home and

Health Department.

If such a weapon is so altered that it is only capable of semi-automatic fire, it may be possible to obtain a Firearm Certificate in respect of it.

Weapons designed to fire tear gas are subject to general prohibition.

(5) *Explosives and ammunition.*

Before gunpowder may be purchased, a permit from the local Chief Officer of Police is required.

Percussion caps may generally be purchased without any licence or permit.

Modern smokeless gunpowder may generally be purchased without any licence or permit, but this is intended for loading shotgun and other cartridges and **must never under any circumstances be used in antique firearms** as it is very liable to blow them up.

Cartridges loaded with single bullets cannot be purchased or held other than by the holder of a Firearm Certificate.

Deactivated cartridges, whose percussion cap has been removed or rendered inert, and whose propellant charge has been removed, may generally be held without certificate. Such ammunition is sometimes advertised, and many people collect it.

Shotgun cartridges may generally be purchased without any certificate, provided that they are loaded with five or more shot, none of which exceeds .36 calibre. If they are loaded with a single bullet, or shot exceeding .36 calibre, a Firearm Certificate is required to purchase them, even though a Shotgun Certificate is required for the weapon which will fire them.

Blank ammunition of less than one inch in bore may be purchased without certificate.

Except under certain special circumstances, a Firearm Certificate is required for the purchase of flare ammunition.

Tear gas ammunition is subject to general prohibition.

(6) *Proof of weapons.*

The *Gun Barrel Proof Acts* are enforced to protect us from inferior weapons. Proof is the compulsory testing of weapons before sale or resale to ensure their safety when in use.

The collector who wishes to fire a gun, but is uncertain whether or not it is in proof, should consult his gunsmith, who may, if necessary, submit the gun for reproof.

Information about the validity of proof marks may be obtained from:

The Proof Master	or The Proof Master
The Proof House	The Gun Barrel Proof
48 Commercial Road	House
London E.1	Banbury Street
	Birmingham 5

(7) *The purchase of guns abroad.*

In the United Kingdom, both the import and the export of firearms are subject to control.

The collector may wish to add to his collection whilst abroad on holiday or a business trip. The advice of the local Customs and Excise Officer should be sought. His advice, in writing, should be kept, so that it can be shown to foreign police and customs officials, and to the customs officer to whom the gun will be declared upon the collector's return.

In some instances it will be necessary to consult the Department of Trade: the local Customs and Excise Officer will advise the collector of this necessity.

When abroad, it is important to buy only from dealers of repute, and to obtain a receipt. The collector must avoid buying guns which cannot legally be exported from the country in which they were bought.

The commercial attaché of that country's embassy ought to be consulted before the journey is made. Many countries have strict laws relating to the export of antiques as well as firearms.

Copies of the following legislation, which affect gun collectors and gun users, may be obtained from branches of Her Majesty's Stationery Office, in Ireland from the Government Publications Sale Office, and elsewhere from the States Greffes or other local authorities.

Great Britain
    The Firearms Act, 1968
    The Gun Barrel Proof Acts, 1868 and 1950

Eire
    The Firearms Acts, 1925, 1964 and 1971
    The Firearms (Proofing) Act, 1968

Jersey
    Loi sur le Porte d'Armes, 1879
    Firearms (Jersey) Law, 1956

Guernsey and Alderney
    Ordre en Conseil, 10 décembre 1921

Isle of Man
    The Firearms Acts, 1947 and 1968
    The Airguns & Shotguns Act, 1968

Accessories

To fire a gun requires ammunition. This may consist of lead bullets and gunpowder, with some flints or percussion caps to ignite the gunpowder, or it may consist of prepared cartridges which are carried in some specially designed container.

The accessories which the collector is most likely to encounter are therefore those objects which are

Fig. 1 *Powder flask made from cow horn, with wooden base and plug, showing typical carved decoration. Dated 1777 on base, probably Scandinavian*

connected with the carriage and preparation of ammunition. When purchasing an antique gun, many collectors like to try to obtain the objects which would have commonly been used with that particular gun.

Usually the first object to be considered is the powder flask, as this is the most frequently encountered. The earliest available flasks were usually made of cow horn, or from the horn or antler of some animal commonly hunted. These are known from the early fifteenth century to the nineteenth century, and some enthusiasts still make their own. The tip of the horn was cut off, and provided with a wooden or bone plug. The base of the horn was enclosed with an oval or rounded piece of wood, nailed or glued into place. Often the horn was flattened somewhat; this was done with steam and pressure. Often it was decorated with engravings of simple geometrical designs, or scenes. More elegantly made examples may have metal fittings.

Some horns have the owner's name or initials, and the date.

A number of powder flasks are found which are made of leather, sometimes limp, but usually boiled so that they are rigid. These often have impressed decorations. The majority of those seen now are of Arab and Indian manufacture.

Some metal powder flasks have probably been produced from the earliest times, but the metal flask does not appear in quantity until the mid-nineteenth century, when technological advances had made mass production practical. These are usually of copper or brass, though zinc, tinned iron and pewter were also used. Gold and silver plated examples are found. Many of these die-stamped metal flasks are still in production for use.

Most of the later flasks will have some sort of cut-off mechanism, usually graduated, so that the correct charge of powder is poured out. The graduations of charge are usually expressed in drachms.

Some nineteenth-century sporting flasks are leather-covered. This was done largely to prevent clanking noises which might startle game.

Similar limp leather flasks, usually of the nineteenth century, are generally shot flasks. These have a distinctive cut-off mechanism, allowing the position of the lid plate to be altered to increase or decrease the charge of shot required. The mechanism is often graduated, the charges being expressed in fractions of an ounce.

When the percussion cap came into general use, cap dispensers were needed. These are generally round, flat containers about the size of a pocket watch. They are generally of brass.

If a military musket, carbine or rifle is bought, the collector may wish to display it with the type of bayonet which would have been in use with it. There

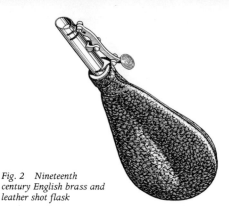

Fig. 2   Nineteenth century English brass and leather shot flask

are large numbers of bayonet collectors, and to cater for them there are specialist dealers in what are termed edged militaria. Unless a seventeenth-century plug-bayonet is required, the correct bayonet for a gun can nearly always be found. It is important to remember that a bayonet is worth a great deal less to bayonet collectors if the scabbard is missing. If the bayonet is only required for display, and the collector does not feel too strongly about having the scabbard, the dealer may often be persuaded to sell the bayonet without the scabbard at a considerably reduced price. Since the scabbards are very often of leather, more bayonets survive than scabbards.

A bullet mould matching the calibre of the gun may be wanted. These are usually of brass or iron. The bullet mould has been in use from the fourteenth century, but the earliest types are only known from

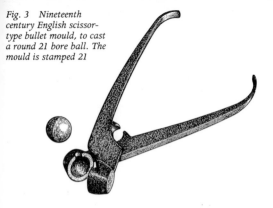

Fig. 3 Nineteenth century English scissor-type bullet mould, to cast a round 21 bore ball. The mould is stamped 21

documentary records. The earliest that the collector may find are of the sixteenth century, but these are very rare. They are usually gang moulds, consisting of a number of hinged leaves. Sometimes the handles were also hinged. A variety of projectiles were cast, from ball the size of the bore, to the larger sizes of shot. During the seventeenth century two-leaved moulds of simpler but similar construction came into use. They are generally more heavily made, and many were capable of casting different sized bullets. Late in the seventeenth century the scissors type of mould came into general popularity. Since these continued to be made until the nineteenth century, the collector has a good chance of finding one. These are simple affairs, usually of wrought iron. The mould itself consists of two opposed cavities, brought together by the scissor action of the handles. A small hole is left through which lead is poured. On the handles of the scissors, near the hinge, are two small opposed blades. These are used to cut the sprue from the bullet. To obtain a decent bullet from one of these moulds, it is best to blacken the cavities of the matrix with the smoke from a candle flame, or to grease them slightly. The later scissor moulds will often have the bore of the gun for which they are intended shown upon them. Thus, if a mould is marked WARRANTED 12, this means that it will cast twelve balls to the pound of lead, and that these balls are intended for a 12 bore gun. Gang moulds, for producing a quantity of full-bore balls or buckshot, continued to be made until the nineteenth century. These are usually long square brass pieces, hinged at one end and having handles at the other. A flat iron plate swivels from the top of the hinge, and is pierced to allow lead to be poured into each matrix. The edges of the piercings are usually bevelled, to allow the top-plate to be used as a sprue-cutter. Similar but smaller moulds for revolver bullets will also be found. These are generally also of brass and iron. These often cast either a spherical ball or a round-nosed flat-based bullet. Moulds of this type are still made. Primitive composite moulds made from soapstone are also encountered, and are usually of Indian or American manufacture. Either the two blocks of soapstone were held together with wooden pegs, holes for which will be seen in the corners of each piece, or the blocks were mounted in larger wooden blocks. If an Indian jezail or torador is purchased, one of these moulds may be added to the collection.

When cartridges were used, it was not necessary to carry a powder horn or shot flask, unless powder was required for priming the pan of a flintlock, or unless the cartridges held ball and wads but no powder. The earliest cartridges consisted simply of a charge of gunpowder wrapped in paper, which was torn open on loading the gun. It is not known how early this practice was introduced. Towards the end of the sixteenth century the bullet seems to have been connected with the cartridge, either by being wrapped in one end of it, or by one end of the cartridge being tied around the sprue of the bullet. Wrapped paper cartridges continued in use well into the nineteenth century. The different types of metallic cartridge invented during the nineteenth century are described in the section of this book which is devoted to early cartridge weapons.

Early paper cartridges have hardly survived, and a collector would be most fortunate to fine one. However, one type of muzzle loading cartridge was used by sportsmen during the nineteenth century. This contained no powder, but a charge of shot between wads. Some are found in which the shot is held in a wire cage. This was intended to keep the pattern of the shot fired tight. If a Victorian percussion shotgun is purchased, the collector may wish to try to find a packet of these cartridges.

An early cartridge box may be encountered. Those for paper cartridges usually consist of some sort of leather or cloth satchel, containing a wooden block, pierced to hold the paper cartridges. Leather and canvas pouches for holding metallic cartridges are usually military, though sporting examples may be found. If the collector buys an early bolt-action rifle, a dealer in militaria may well be able to supply him with the correct cartridge pouch.

The bandolier seems to have appeared early in the sixteenth century. This was a leather or fabric belt worn over one shoulder and under the opposite arm, from which were suspended a number of containers, each containing a charge of powder. These containers were usually made of boxwood, but copper, brass, boiled leather, pewter, potin and latten were probably all used. In Western Europe the bandolier was abandoned before the end of the seventeenth century, in favour of paper cartridges. Examples available to collectors are likely to be of Eastern European, Asiatic or African origin. In addition to its charge boxes, the bandolier may also have carried a priming flask for touch powder, and a limp leather bag for bullets.

The more modern type of bandolier, for sporting cartridges, is still made. Victorian examples may be found. Bandoliers were also used for military cartridges, especially by cavalry. These also may be found.

Many carbines and pistols have been carried in holsters. It is thought that these came into use for wheel-lock pistols, early in the sixteenth century. Holsters may be conveniently divided into four types. The saddle holster for long pistols is probably the earliest. When the revolver came into use, during the mid-nineteenth century, the saddle holster was replaced by the belt holster. At about the same time holsters for carrying carbines on horseback seem to have been introduced. Similar holsters for sporting guns are sometimes found. When the smaller automatic pistols were introduced, holsters were designed to allow them to be carried under the shoulder. Holsters are usually of leather or fabric, but composite wooden and leather holsters were made for some of the earlier automatic pistols. The wooden part of the holster could be attached to the butt of the pistol, allowing it to be used as a carbine. The collector of the more modern military pistols will usually be able to find the correct holster for them, often with the correct date stamped into the leather. Carbine holsters can sometimes be found for Victorian military carbines. Holsters for pistols are very much more difficult to locate, and the collector may well be offered Eastern European or Middle Eastern specimens.

Some weapons required a specific tool to be carried with them. The wheel-lock requires a spanner to wind up the spring in the action: these spanners are a rarity. Users of percussion weapons often kept a nipple wrench, in case of snapped, chipped and mangled nipples. Nipple wrenches are not uncommon.

Some variety of other accessories may be obtained. Like the fisherman, the sporting shot or target shot often loves to surround himself with all manner of impedimenta. Anything may be purchased, if a gunsmith or a magazine article persuades him that game will be added to his bag, or a point to his score. A visit to a shooting competition may illustrate this. Such people are no more or less common now than they were a hundred years ago. Perusal of Victorian sporting goods catalogues can be most informative, when the collector wishes to ascertain the use of some mysterious object which has turned up.

Forgeries and Copies

The forgery of antique firearms commenced towards the end of the nineteenth century, at a time when many of the largest and best collections were being built up. The interest in antique firearms was then relatively new, and the forgers had previously devoted most of their attention to the falsification of ancient edged weapons and armour.

The earlier forgers concentrated largely on wheel-lock weapons. In many cases they obtained existing genuine guns, and lavishly embellished them with precious metals and engraving. Many collectors of the time were generally interested in the fine arts, and the forger usually sought to turn a simple military gun, or a slightly decorated sporting gun, into a work of art.

By the second decade of the present century, the earlier snaphaunce and flintlock weapons were commanding sufficiently high prices to interest the forger. Guns of inferior quality were worked upon, so that they appeared to be of better quality, or earlier in date.

33

The original makers' names, if present, were erased, and those of well known gunsmiths engraved on the locks and sometimes on the barrels. Many weapons were engraved with inscriptions associating them with some well-known historical event or person.

As percussion weapons have become more valuable, these also have been worked upon. Earlier percussion guns which had originally been converted from flintlock have been converted back to flintlock. In the case of a rare flintlock weapon, this might be regarded as a legitimate repair: whether or not it is legitimate depends upon the intention of the person doing the conversion. Common percussion pistols, such as revolvers, have been worked upon to turn them into presentation models. A common American revolver might be turned into an earlier product by the erasing of part of the serial number, or it might be turned into a Confederate weapon of the American Civil War by having its frame changed, its makers' name altered, and perhaps a spurious inscription added.

Flintlock, percussion and cartridge weapons, especially when found in a bad state of repair, have been altered to resemble guns used by American Indians, by the addition of brass-headed tacks and leather barrel bands.

Flintlock and percussion sporting guns of inferior quality, made well into this century for the African market, have been worked upon to make them appear older and more important guns. Many flintlock and percussion guns are still made, particularly in Italy, Japan and Belgium, for the use of people who wish to use such guns. Forgers remove the modern markings and age these guns.

Obsolete European weapons have been available in quantity from India and the Middle East for some time. These weapons are rebuilt from old parts, and often new parts, in Europe, the Middle East and India. Once

34

again, whether this is repair or forgery, is entirely a matter of intent. Indian matchlock and percussion weapons will be found which are outright copies, containing no original parts. These were made largely as decorations, for tourists to buy as souvenirs, but many are finding their way onto the antiques market.

There is little that the forger can do to increase the value of a modern cartridge weapon. It may be converted into a presentation piece by engraving and plating with a precious metal, or simply by the addition of an inscribed silver plate. Some mechanical feature may be added or altered, to make the weapon appear to be a prototype or experimental piece.

Indian and Afghan longarms, jezails and toradors are often embellished with brass shim and mother-of-pearl inlay, to make them appear more interesting or more decorative.

All forgeries should be examined most carefully. The collector should never simply not look at something because it is an obvious forgery. Even the most blatant forgeries can demonstrate some feature which will be found on a number of other forgeries, and this feature may well be less obvious on the example next encountered.

The collector may never become sufficiently experienced always to spot a forgery. There are a number of guns in important collections, aspects of whose authenticity have been hotly debated by experts over many years.

The feel of a genuine piece can only be obtained by handling as many pieces as possible. This experience cannot be obtained otherwise, and every available gun should be examined, whether or not it is of interest.

When a piece has been handled, and feels satisfactory, it must be examined more closely. Firstly, does the action work, and if it doesn't, why doesn't it? The dealer should know this. The action of a gun should not be worked until the owner's consent has been obtained. The fall of a dog or hammer, or the return of a spring-loaded bolt, should be impeded by the fingers, otherwise broken cocks, mangled nipples, and broken firing pins may result. Much of the damage seen on antique firearms is the result of bad handling.

The action must be examined carefully. Some part may be missing, such as the top jaw of the dog on a flintlock, or the nipple of a percussion gun. In such cases the cost and availability of a replacement must be taken into consideration. Some part may have been replaced. In such cases the metal may be of a different texture or colour, and the style of the engraving may not match that on other parts of the gun. The bolt of a rifle may not have the same serial number as the barrel.

The visible metal of the barrel must then be examined. If there are discrepancies of colour or texture, there must be come explanation for this: perhaps a barrel band is missing.

The stock must be examined, particularly at those points where the breech of the barrel and the action are let into it. Either the barrel or the action may have been replaced, and in that case are unlikely to fit exactly. If the stock is dried out, some allowance must be made for shrinkage which may have taken place, and have drawn the woodwork away from the metal. Such shrinkage is quite distinctive, and once a genuine example has been encountered, it should be easily recognized.

The brass and iron furniture must be compared. Perhaps the gun originally had an iron trigger guard or butt plate, and these have been replaced with brass to make the gun appear more decorative. Perhaps the original trigger guard or one of the ramrod pipes was missing or broken, and has been replaced. In this case it is quite likely that the texture and colour of the original metal will differ from that of the original parts which remain. This is particularly the case with brass, which is an alloy having many different shades of colour.

The metal parts should be looked at together and overall. Perhaps some reblueing or rebrowning has been done. The original blueing or browning will have deteriorated most around the nipple or touch hole, and also where the weapon would naturally have rubbed against a holster or box. A weapon which has been rebrowned or reblued will not have these characteristics. A particular sign to watch for is reblueing over the pitted area around a nipple.

If a gun is cased, is the case original or not? The cases for pistols and sporting guns are common and were made in fairly standard ways, so it should be easy to handle enough of them to obtain a good idea of what they ought to look like. There may be a maker's label inside the lid of the box, and this should correspond with the maker's name which appears upon the gun. If it does not, the label may be that of the original retailer of the gun, who may not have made the gun itself. This may be clear from the written content of the label.

The case may contain accessories, in particular powder flask and bullet mould. The powder flask may be a reproduction, as they are still made for people who use them. The bullet mould should be of the same calibre as the gun: it may also be a reproduction.

The gun and accessories in their case should be looked at together and overall. If they all belong together, they should fit exactly. There will often be abrasions to the fabric lining of the case, where sights, hammers and trigger guards have rubbed against it. These should tally with the shape and detail of the gun.

The gun may have a silver-capped butt, or the case may have silver corners. Such pieces of silver may be hall-marked, and hall-marks should tally with each other and with the date of the gun.

A useful thing to do, if the dealer consents, is to

remove the action and the barrel from the stock. Any fresh cutting is suspect. All the parts should fit snugly. If the action is taken off, the springs, in particular the mainspring, should be examined for cracks.

An antique dealer with a valuable piece may quite reasonably not permit it to be stripped, for fear that damage might result. On the other hand, a gunsmith from whom a gun is being bought as an antique or for use, will usually be willing to strip the gun down to show the buyer how this is done.

It must always be remembered that a gun was intended to be used, whether the collector himself intends to use it or not. It may have had a long life and been lovingly cared for, or it may have had a long rough life in a farmhand's cottage or a series of government arsenals in different countries. In either case parts may well have been replaced as they wore out. The gun may have had a new barrel, perhaps more than once, and it may have been converted from one system of ignition to another. A military weapon may have been cut down for use as a sporting gun when it became obsolete militarily. Only by handling a quantity of guns can the collector learn to distinguish early, later, and modern alterations. It is up to the individual to decide what degree of perfection he requires in his collection.

Restoration and Repairs

The first and most important thing to do, when acquiring an antique gun from any source, is to make sure that it is not loaded. Large numbers of guns, in particular percussion muzzle-loading pistols, are loaded when found. People very often kept loaded pistols in their houses, and, since they seldom had need to fire them, they were left loaded for years on end, until finally forgotten and lost in an attic or shed. Careless sportsmen put away guns loaded. A gun picked up on a battlefield and brought home as a trophy may be loaded. Even guns sold off by government arsenals may be loaded. A couple of years ago the writer purchased an Indian Army version of an Enfield Pattern 1853 musket. This was found to contain five charges on top of one another, despite the fact that it must have passed through at least two salerooms specializing in arms, past two customs and excise organizations, and lastly through the hands of a registered firearms dealer. Had a power tool been applied to the breech or nipple, or had a percussion cap been fired to test the strength of the hammer, the gun barrel could have exploded with something like the effect of a hand grenade. On another occasion the writer was cleaning an 1898 pattern Mauser bolt action rifle. The action had jammed, perhaps on the battlefield where it was picked up. Although the magazine was empty, there was a cartridge in the breech.

It is quite simple to establish whether or not a gun is loaded, and there is no excuse for keeping what may be a dangerous weapon for any longer than it takes to find out. If the gun is a breech loader, open the breech and look. If it is an automatic weapon, take out the magazine and put it down, and then work the slide or cocking piece sufficiently to reveal the breech or to eject any cartridge that may be chambered. If it is a muzzle-loading weapon, or a breech-loader with a jammed breech, pass a wooden rod or a ramrod down the barrel as far as it will go, then mark the ramrod with a felt tipped pen or something similar at the point where it emerges from the muzzle. Take out the ramrod, and see if the length of it which has been in the barrel corresponds with the outside measurement of the barrel from breech to muzzle. If these measurements do not correspond, there is a reasonable chance that the gun is loaded.

If the gun is a breech-loader which is liable to be

loaded with a metallic cartridge, it must be taken to a gunsmith. If it is a muzzle-loader, the barrel must be taken off, stood breech-downwards in a bucket of hot water, and the barrel filled with boiling water. This will turn the wads into a mush which will wash out in the end, and will dissolve the saltpetre in the gunpowder and render it inert. This treatment, repeated several times, perhaps over a few days, will generally wash out the top wad or patch sufficiently to allow the ball or charge of shot to be shaken out. Further washing will remove the remaining wadding and powder. If it does not, a worm must be used. This is a tool resembling a corkscrew or gimlet, which screws onto the end of a ramrod. The tip of it is screwed into the lead ball, allowing it to be drawn out. This must be done slowly and with care, as jerky movements will tear the lead, and it may be difficult to get further grips with the worm. If the barrel cannot be removed, the gun should be taken to a gunsmith, who may either be able to remove the breech plug, or may be able to draw the charge without removing the breech plug.

Occasionally weapons will be found which defy the ramrod test, because they have some sort of patent breech, containing a constriction or a standing pillar. For this reason it is best to use a proper narrow steel ramrod, with which the breech can be felt, rather than a thicker wooden rod. Most dealers will have a heap of odd ramrods, one of which can be bought cheaply. A long musket ramrod is best, as it can be used for everything except enormous punt guns and wall pieces. If there is any uncertainty whatsoever as to whether a gun is loaded or not, it should be treated as loaded. Even when it is known not to be loaded, it should **never** be pointed at anyone.

Having established that his gun is not loaded, the collector must decide whether it requires any re-storation or repair. Should he have any doubts about his competence to perform any repair or restoration, the gun should be left alone. A bad repair may render the gun worth less than it was had it been left alone. It is very disappointing to make a bad repair which cannot be remedied, and just has to be tolerated. Gunsmiths will often repair antique guns for collectors.

There are several ways of obtaining experience. Perhaps the best, if it is possible to do it, is to attend one of the courses arranged in many areas by museums and local authorities. These provide experience in the restoration of all manner of antiquities. The amateur has to contend not only with iron, steel and wood, but with brass fittings, metal inlaid with other metals such as brass, copper, silver and gold, and with wood inlaid with ivory, mother-of-pearl, metals and other woods. Therefore the wider the experience he has of antiquities as a whole, the better he will be able to restore and repair guns in his own collection. If a course cannot be attended, the next best way of obtaining experience is to obtain some terrible old guns which are only fit to be put in the dustbin, and whose absolute destruction is unimportant. The complete rebuilding of a ruin, or the attempt, will teach a great deal that cannot otherwise be taught, and is very satisfying if successful. If the attempt is not successful, the experience has still been gained, and this experience and the knowledge gained of personal capabilities is well worth the cost of some unpleasant relics.

Deciding how much to repair and restore is a matter of personal taste. It may be desired to restore the weapon as nearly as possible to the condition it was in when new, but most collectors seem to desire nothing more than the careful cleaning of a gun, and the minimum of repairs done, sufficient only to return it to working order. When repairing a valuable weapon, it may be important to consider the preferences of collectors as a whole, rather than personal preferences,

41

as one day the gun may need to be sold or exchanged.

The difference between restoration and forgery is simply one of intent. It is generally acceptable that a gun should be restored as nearly as reasonable to its original condition, but there can be no justification whatever for additions, alterations or embellishments. It would probably be generally accepted that it would be ethical to collect the parts of a very rare gun, such as a sixteenth century English matchlock, to obtain the measurements of a surviving specimen, and then to build the weapon. If this is done by a reputable gunsmith, he will stamp his name, that of the city where he works, and perhaps the date, so deeply into the parts that he can be sure that it will be very difficult indeed for the gun to be used in a future fraud. On the other hand, it would generally be frowned upon to build a common Victorian musket from odd parts, unless the intention was to produce a gun for sporting use and it was clearly marked as a reproduction. It would additionally bear modern proof-marks.

If it is decided that a gun requires attention, it must be stripped. Some idea must first be had of how it works and how it was put together in the first place. This may be obtained either by examining the insides of other weapons, or from some instruction manual. It is very irritating to undo a couple of screws on the action of, say, a Martini–Enfield rifle, and then to have miscellaneous pieces of ironmongery of unknown purpose impelled around the room. Assembling an action of this type, which cannot be seen as it is inside a box, without some knowledge of how it works, is about as easy as knitting in the dark.

Usually, the weapon to be stripped will be a muzzle-loader or an early breech-loader. The first thing to remove is the lock. This is done by unscrewing one or more screws which pass through the stock. It is important to have a screwdriver of exactly the right size, and with the right shaped tip to its blade. It is best to have a quantity of old screwdrivers which can be filed down to fit each type of screw encountered. If the screw cannot be unscrewed, it may have to be drilled out.

The barrel must be removed after the lock. There will usually be a screw through the tang at the breech, into the butt. This must be removed first, unless it is not connected to the barrel. It may only be holding a plate into which the breech plug at the base of the barrel is hooked. The barrel is then held on by pins, wedges, or bands. If the stock is clean enough, the barrel pins can be spotted and driven out carefully with a drift. Great care is vital, as the pins may very well be rusted into the stock, in which case an incautious blow may tear out a chunk of wood on the other side of the stock. Wedges seldom rust in very firmly. One end of the wedge is flanged, and these flanges are intended to enable the wedges to be pulled out. If they do not come out easily, the wedges should be driven out a little from the other side of the stock with a screwdriver, until the flanges are exposed sufficiently to permit a good grip. The wedges should never be levered out by the flanges, as this will dent the woodwork and wedge-plates. Barrel bands are usually retained by a screw at the base, which can be quite stubborn. If they cannot be unscrewed they can be drilled out, if some replacements are available. If they are drilled out, it is quite likely that the threads in the barrel bands will have to be retapped. Oriental weapons may have barrel bands of brass sheet, wire, or leather. Before these are removed the possibility of replacing them must be considered.

The trigger guard, butt-plate and other furniture is usually screwed into the wood, though some butt-plates may be glued on. Again, it is important to have screwdrivers of the correct dimensions, or mangled

43

screws will be the result. Screws of these types are much more easily replaced than those pertaining more nearly to the mechanism of the gun, but the original screws should be preserved whenever possible.

Now that the gun is reduced to its component parts, the collector will have to decide which parts are missing, damaged beyond repair, or simply need cleaning.

Quantities of replacement parts are commercially available. These have to be filed and polished to shape. It is usually beyond the expertise of the amateur to make a new spring, so the advice of a gunsmith, locksmith or springsmith should be sought. If possible, the mechanism should be left with the smith so that he can make the best spring for it. Dirty parts may be left to stand for a while in methylated spirit, paraffin, or acetone. The latter is particularly useful where a quantity of old grease is involved. The parts may then be cleaned with fine emery paper, or wire wool dipped in spirit.

Cleaning the barrel will introduce the collector to two sorts of rust, loose red rust, and rather harder black rust. The loose red rust is best removed with fine emery paper. The hard black rust, if there is pitting beneath it, is probably best left alone, as it is chemically quite stable and will not cause any further deterioration. If there is no pitting, or little pitting, beneath the rust, it can be removed by using emery paper in series from coarser to finer. The finest jewellers' emery paper can give a mirror finish.

Stocks will generally require cleaning. They may be dried out, covered with old varnish and dirt, or slimy with old oil from countless arsenals. If a stock is dry and cracked, the crack must be dealt with first. This depends on the nature of the crack, and it is best to seek the advice of the nearest carpenter or cabinet-maker who specializes in the restoration of antique furniture.

Failing that, the gunsmith may be able to help. The dry stock should be carefully sanded down until a smooth finish is obtained, and all traces of old varnishes removed. It can then be rubbed over with boiled linseed oil until the appearance is satisfactory. The linseed should be allowed to dry between each application. The fewest problems are presented by stocks which merely have an accumulation of old varnishes and dirt. Much of this can usually be wiped off with linseed oil, or in more stubborn cases linseed oil and wire wool. Stocks which have been in military stores for a hundred years, and are thoroughly impregnated with oil, will need thoroughly rubbing over with spirit and wire wool, probably over a period of weeks or months. Stubborn examples may be pared down with a knife. A knife with a straight edge, held vertically to the stock, should be used. This may well result in the loss of the arsenal marks, which may or may not be desirable, depending on how appropriate they are to the type of weapon, and how meaningful they are to the collector. It is sometimes possible to pare round the arsenal marks, but unfortunately it is often found that the earliest and most interesting marks are the most lightly impressed. After finishing with the knife, progressively finer degrees of sandpaper and emery paper should be used, until the stock is perfectly smooth. It may then be found that oils continue to exude from the wood, especially in the region of the action. These have to be cleaned away with spirit, until the stock is sufficiently dry to be treated with boiled linseed oil.

Dents in barrels are difficult to raise without exactly the right tools. Generally these appear on thin-barrelled sporting weapons, and the gunsmith will be able to raise them, as the barrels of modern sporting weapons can also be thin and are sometimes dented.

Dents in stocks can often be raised with steam. A

45

piece of cloth is soaked in hot water, placed over the dent, and a hot iron applied. In the case of very oily stocks this should not be done until the bulk of the oil has been removed, as the removal of the oil will quite often cause the dents to raise themselves. Most dents in oily stocks are caused after the weapons have become oily, by other weapons banging against them. The dents may therefore consist of bends in the fibres of the wood rather than breakages, and when the wood regains something of its original texture, the bends in the fibres may straighten themselves.

Metals such as silver, copper and base gold, when inlaid into wooden or metal parts of the gun, will often be tarnished. It can be cleaned initially with wire wool and spirit, if badly tarnished, and subsequently with normal metal polishes. Wire wools impregnated with soap are useful. Care must be taken with Indian barrels, which may not be inlaid, but gilt. This is relatively thin, and has become thinner with use. It can be replaced with the type of gold leaf used in bookbinding, but the replacement will be fragile, and it will be difficult to match the colour of the original remaining gold. The surfaces which bore the gilt will be rough, either cross-hatched or etched with an acid. The gold leaf is stacked, each leaf being separated from the last by a leaf of goldbeaters' skin. This is made from the conjunctive tissues of animals, and should be available from jewellers' wholesalers. The pile is then beaten with a flat-headed wooden mawl, very thoroughly and for some time. When the gold has taken on the steel, it is burnished with an oiled steel needle, or the round edge of some other steel implement which is smooth, and then heated. It is then heated and burnished again. Silver leaf may be applied in the same way, but silver leaf is very much more difficult to obtain than gold.

The collector may want to lacquer some of the metal surfaces, to avoid the necessity of frequent cleaning. If this is to be done, the lacquer should be tested on some other similar metal surface first, and it should be established how easily such a lacquer can be removed if necessary, and with which solvents. An inferior lacquer may cause surfaces to appear dull.

It may be decided that the original blueing or browning should be restored. A variety of substances are commercially available. Most of them are rather poisonous and should be kept under lock and key: selenious acid, for example, may cause blindness. Before any of these substances are applied, the surfaces must be cleaned thoroughly with some solvent such as acetone, or with a strong detergent. New parts can be blued by keeping them at red heat in a metal container, in which they must be completely buried in bone or leather charcoal, for about an hour. Small parts such as screws can be blued by heating them until red hot, and then throwing them into oil.

Once again it must be emphasized that if a collector is not sure whether or not he is capable of restoring a valuable piece, he should leave it alone.

The Literature (see Bibliography, p. 189)

To build up a worthwhile collection of firearms, an amount of knowledge is required. All too often the collector avoids buying books, and subscribing to magazines and auction catalogues, in order to save money which he intends to spend on his collection. This may well prove to be a false economy. Weapons may be bought which would not have been bought had the collector the opportunity to read about them. Without books, little information can be obtained about the history and performance of different types of gun. Without magazines and auction catalogues, it is almost impossible to have a clear idea of prices outside a limited area.

Many gunsmiths sell books. Most large bookshops

have some section devoted to militaria or arms and armour, in which books relating to firearms will be found. There are a few booksellers who specialize in books on arms and armour.

A few antiquarian and second-hand book dealers specialize in military books. It is not always easy to find them, as many of them trade from their homes, and send out periodical lists. These dealers are well worth finding, as they often list books relating to firearms. The local antiquarian or second-hand book dealer will probably have a list of dealers, published frequently, which describes the specialities of each dealer. It can also be worthwhile to visit book fairs, which take place in most parts of the country once or twice a year. The local antiquarian book dealer will normally have information about the date and locality of such fairs.

Apart from antiquarian books relating to firearms in general, one category of book is collectable in its own right. If, for instance, an Enfield rifled musket of the 1853 pattern is acquired, the collector may wish to have the instruction manual relating to it. In this instance, it would be entitled *Extracts from Regulations for conducting Musketry Instruction of the Army*, or *Drill and Rifle Instruction for the Corps of Rifle Volunteers*. Such manuals are usually found listed under the title *Musketry Regulations* or *Musketry Instruction*, and can usually be obtained quite cheaply. Some earlier and rarer books of this type have been reprinted. If the gun is obtained, the reprint of the manual should not be rejected because the original cannot be found. For taking the gun to pieces and cleaning it, or restoring it, the reprint will be no less useful.

A considerable amount of information may be gleaned from specialist auction catalogues. Even if the auctioneer is too distant to visit, his catalogues are a worthwhile addition to any library. Many of the major London auctioneers sometimes have arms sales, and it is possible to subscribe to the catalogues of these only. Important provincial auctioneers whose catalogues should not be missed are Weller & Dufty Ltd., of 141 Bromsgrove Street, Birmingham 5, and Wallis & Wallis, of 1 Albion Street, Lewes, Sussex.

The collector may not wish to overlook books about military history. If a nineteenth century musket is obtained, which is known to have been issued to a particular regiment or volunteer force, it may be interesting to have a history of that force.

There are a few magazines which cater for both the gun user and the gun collector. From time to time these contain articles describing some type of antique gun in greater detail that may conveniently be found elsewhere. Through their advertising columns, they may be a great help in adding to a collection, or in disposing of items which are no longer wanted.

Sometimes a collector will acquire an eighteenth- or nineteenth-century weapon made in his own town, and may want to obtain more information about the gunsmith who made it. It may be that the local museum or library will have a series of directories and registers of voters. From these, the period when the gunsmith was working can be established. Once a period of working years is known for the gunsmith, it may be interesting to peruse local magazines and newspapers of that period and to make copies of advertisements and other information relating to the gunsmith. Such newspapers and magazines may be found in the museum or library. The county archivist may be able to help.

Certain dealers specialize in manuscripts, pamphlets and other printed ephemera. It can be useful to find such a dealer and to ask him to keep anything relating to firearms. He may not have any other customers for such documents. If there is such a dealer in the area, an antiquarian or second-hand book dealer may know where to find him.

Periodicals intended for museum staff, such as *Studies in Conservation*, may contain articles of use to the collector who wishes to restore or repair his guns.

Public Collections
Most museums and a number of art galleries have some firearms in their collections. In many cases they will not be on display, but in reserve or store. If the curator is approached, he may allow weapons not on display to be examined.

Regimental museums and military or naval establishments sometimes have collections of weapons which may be viewed on application. Some national and private arms manufacturers have reference collections.

HAND CANNONS AND MATCHLOCKS

The place and date of origin of the hand cannon are not known. Documentary references are rare, and surviving examples still rarer. It is quite possible that the hand cannon appeared at about the same time as the cannon proper, and became widely known in Europe during the fourteenth century. The earliest European record relating to the manufacture of firearms is a Florentine government document of 1326, in which certain people are authorized to make metal cannon and iron cannon balls for the defence of the Florentine Republic. In England, Exchequer Accounts of 1333–34 show gunpowder to have been in store.

The possibility of making cannons depends upon the recognition of the propellant properties of gunpowder. This substance consists, by weight, of approximately 75 parts saltpetre or nitre, 10 parts of sulphur, and 15 parts of charcoal. When it was discovered is not known, but it is thought that the component chemicals were used in Chinese incendiary mixtures of the eleventh century. It seems that these formulae were brought to the west by Arabs, and that true gunpowder may have been developed in Europe during the second quarter of the thirteenth century.

Earlier firearms in the west were incendiary devices. The invention of an incendiary mixture known as Greek Fire is attributed to a seventh century architect and chemist Callinicus, who is sometimes said to have been a native of Baalbek in the Lebanon. The best developed of the incendiary firearms were thick pottery grenades, which were widely used in the Middle East.

Fig. 4   Medieval Arab pottery grenade, found in Palestine

The first true hand cannons seems to have consisted of a short iron or bronze barrel, solid or plugged at the rear, and fixed to a wooden stave or tiller. The firer poured a charge of gunpowder into the muzzle, rammed down a wad on top of it, and then rammed the projectile down on top of the wad. The weapon was then propped up, or its stock rested against the body or under an arm, and was steadied by one hand while a smouldering tinder or match was held to the touch hole with the other. When this type of weapon was produced is not known. The earliest document illustrating one is a manuscript of Konrad Kyeser's *Belliforte*, dated 1405, in Göttingen University Library. There is no reason to suppose that the type of weapon was new then.

The earlier gunpowders were often quite inefficient: this is known as a number of formulas have survived in which the proportions of the components are given. All

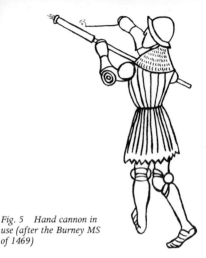

Fig. 5   Hand cannon in use (after the Burney MS of 1469)

manner of weird and useless components, such as camphor and mercury, were added at various times. But to be useful in war, a weapon did not have to be efficient to be effective. A battle could be won, not by the number of men killed or wounded, but by the number of men and horses frightened.

A variety of projectiles seem to have been used; rounded stones, lead bullets, and short arrows were probably the most usual. The short arrows were probably similar or identical to the quarrels fired from crossbows.

The first mechanical contrivance for placing the lit match in the touch hole is known as the matchlock (*see* **6**). This consists of an arm holding the match, called a serpentine, which is lowered to the touch hole by

Fig. 6   Action of a 17th century Japanese snapping matchlock gun. The serpentine is cocked against the external mainspring, and the priming pan cover is swung forward

leverage, or dropped into the touch hole by a mechanism which releases it.

It is not certainly known when or where the matchlock was developed, but records show it to have been in use in central Europe during the latter part of the fifteenth century. The earliest examples would have been hand cannons with an S-shaped metal arm controlling the match. An early development would have been a concave priming pan to hold powder around the touch hole.

At about the same time a type of stock was introduced which supported the barrel of the gun from beneath, and had a rudimentary butt which enabled the gun to be fired from the shoulder.

These two developments made some degree of accuracy possible. The earliest recorded shooting competition took place at Geneva in 1474, and such competitions became popular throughout central Europe. Shooting Guilds were organized, but declined because of the disturbances of the Thirty Years War.

Rifling seems to have been invented late in the fifteenth century. Augustus Kotter of Nuremberg,

Gaspard Kollner of Vienna and an unknown Leipzig gunsmith are all credited with the invention, which seems to have taken place in south Germany or Austria. Rifling consists of a series of spiral grooves cut into the barrel of a gun. This imparts a spinning motion to the bullet, keeping it on a more accurate course. The reasons for the effects of rifling were not clearly understood. Some believed that the small devils that normally cause a bullet to miss the target were unable to remain seated on a spinning ball. In an experimental competition organized by the Bishop of Mainz in 1547, the competitors were given blessed silver bullets and ordinary lead bullets. The silver bullets failed to reach the target, since, being harder than lead, they could not engage the rifling. It was concluded that rifle bullets were guided by devils.

Gunpowder was improved throughout this period, and the alchemical and magical ingredients left out.

The best matchcord was made from flax and hemp tow. This is a fibrous substance combed out when the flax or hemp is being prepared for the manufacture of textiles. It was spun into cords. If well made, 4 or 5 inches of this cord would glow for an hour.

The matchlock remained a standard military weapon throughout the sixteenth and seventeenth centuries. It gradually replaced the long-bow and the cross-bow during the sixteenth century, and was itself superseded by flintlock arms in the seventeenth. By the early eighteenth century it was probably obsolete everywhere in Europe.

European explorers and military forces made the matchlock well known throughout the world. It continued to be made in India, China, Japan and Central Asia until the nineteenth century.

Hand Cannon

Overall length: 30 cm
Calibre: 30 mm

This small bronze gun was found at Loshult, Småland, Sweden, and is believed to have been made during the early fourteenth century.

It is not clear how the gun could have been held for firing. Perhaps it was propped up on a convenient surface. Similar but probably larger weapons are shown in English manuscripts of Walter de Milemete, dated 1326–1327. These are mounted on structures resembling tables, described in contemporary records as trunks. The illustrations show arrows being fired.

If it is a hand-gun at all, and not just a small cannon, this weapon may be the earliest known.   NHMS

Hand Cannon

Overall length, surviving part: 19.5 cm
Barrel length: 10 cm
Calibre: 21 mm

The bronze gun illustrated is believed to be of German manufacture, and to have been made during the late fourteenth century. It was found in the sea off Mörkö, Södermanland, Sweden.

The hexagonal barrel and breech bear religious inscriptions. The chased bronze head behind the touch hole might have protected the firer from sparks. Since the original stock or tiller has not survived, we do not know how far away the firer's face would have been.

The fin extending below the breech has been described as a recoil stop, but such weapons may not have had a significant recoil when used with the crude gunpowders of the day. It is quite probable that the fin was to help steady the gun against a wall or the side of a boat, or to hold it firmly against a rest.

This is one of the oldest guns known, and is perhaps the most finely made example to have survived. NHMS

Hand Cannon

Overall length: 161 cm
Barrel length: 21 cm
Bore: 18 mm

This wrought-iron gun was found in the ruins of Vedelspang Castle, Schleswig-Holstein, Germany. The castle was built in 1416, and destroyed in 1426: the gun is presumed to date from the same time, and to be Danish or German.

The hook-like recoil stop enabled the gun to be steadied on a wall for aiming. Not all these weapons seem to have had touch holes. Several manuscripts suggest that some were loaded to the muzzle with superimposed charges, and ignited from the muzzle. They would have fired somewhat in the manner of a Roman Candle firework.

A manuscript of 1420, formerly in Vienna, shows soldiers using these guns. The right hand grasps the stock immediately behind the breech, the butt being crooked in the left arm. A drawing dated 1449, also formerly in Vienna, shows a horseman firing with the butt resting against his breastplate. Sometimes it appears that such weapons must have been ignited by a second person, but the slow and inefficient powders of the day probably enabled the firer to light his piece, and then aim it quickly while it was fizzing, if he could not light it from the aiming position. TC

English Matchlock

Overall length, (average): 72 in. (musket) 59 in.
(caliver)
Barrel length, (average): 54 in. (musket) 42 in.
(caliver)

The smooth-bore muzzle loader illustrated was a standard military weapon of the third quarter of the seventeenth century. The pike shown beside it is the rest from which it was fired.

The serpentine is cocked against a spring on the inside of the lock-plate. To fire the gun, the priming pan cover is moved to the right, and pressure on the trigger releases the serpentine, which pushes the match into the priming pan.

These are the first British military weapons to be generally equipped with a trigger as we now know it. Earlier examples have the bar or sear trigger which appears on Indian and Far Eastern arms until the late nineteenth century. The provision of this type of trigger enables the firer to take a better grip and more accurate aim, and the trigger guard provides some degree of safety against accidental discharge. Only a fore-sight is provided, as on a modern shot gun.

Alongside the flintlock and the wheel-lock, weapons of this type were used in the Civil War, and were almost certainly in the majority. Between the Restoration of the Monarchy and the end of the seventeenth century, the matchlock was gradually superseded by the flintlock. Better quality matchlocks were converted to flintlock, but many matchlocks doubtless survived as sporting weapons well into the eighteenth century.

The charges for matchlocks were carried on bandoliers, in a dozen or more tubes made of horn or wood, and covered with leather. The lead balls were carried in a separate bag.   SI

Indian Matchlock

Overall lengths: 100–225 cm
Barrel lengths: 60–130 cm

The weapon shown is a muzzle-loading smoothbore gun of about 20 bore. It is probably of the eighteenth century, but uninscribed weapons of this type are difficult to date. Some examples are relatively modern.

The skeleton trigger bar is held down by a leaf spring inside the butt. When the trigger bar is squeezed towards the butt, the arm of the serpentine is lowered into the priming pan. The match held by the serpentine ignites the powder in the priming pan. This passes fire to the breech, firing the gun.

Most weapons of this type are equipped with priming pan covers. Beneath the priming pan there is often a tube, containing a needle on a chain. This is for picking out the touch-hole when it becomes foul.

Bead fore-sights and notch rear-sights are generally provided: in this case the fore-sight bead is of copper.

The barrel is held onto the stock by four brass bands: the fifth band, behind the action, seems to be purely decorative. The remaining furniture is of iron and steel, boldly pierced for decoration. The breech and muzzle of the barrel are deeply engraved with highly stylized foliage and birds.

A ramrod is provided: often these were carried separately.

Chinese Matchlock

Overall lengths: 100–200 cm
Barrel lengths: 75–125 cm

The example shown is a muzzle-loading smooth-bore gun of about 24 bore. It is probably of the nineteenth century, but weapons of this type are very difficult to date, as they seem to have changed little during the period 1600–1900.

The mechanism is extremely simple. A leaf spring in the butt holds the serpentine erect and the trigger bar down. The priming pan has a sliding iron cover. To fire the gun, the pan cover is swung open, and pressure on the trigger bar below the butt brings the lit match in the serpentine down into the powder, until fire is communicated to the breech.

The pierced square extension of the fore-end stock allows a bipod or monopod to be attached: these guns tend to be rather long and unwieldy, and can be most accurately fired from a bipod. Otherwise, the gun is held with the butt as a pistol grip in front of the right cheek, or from the shoulder or chest.

There is an aperture rear-sight but no fore-sight.

The barrel is held on only by thin brass strip, which is also used for strengthening the stock at the ends and around the breech and pan. The stock is lacquered red overall.

Similar guns, with straighter stocks, leather barrel bands and leather pan covers, are usually Mongolian or Tibetan.

It is presumed that weapons of this type became known to the Chinese by the overland trade routes from Turkey and Russia, perhaps in the sixteenth century.

Japanese Snapping Matchlock

Overall length (average): 125 cm
Barrel length (average): 100 cm

The gun illustrated is a .50 calibre smooth-bore muzzle loader of the mid-seventeenth century.

The mechanism is of a type which had a limited popularity in sixteenth century Europe, and was introduced to Japan by the Portuguese in 1542. It remained in production with little variation until the mid-nineteenth century, when it was briefly superseded by percussion weapons.

The serpentine is cocked against the spring seen on the outside of the lock-plate. It is shown in the fired position, having been released by pressure on the button trigger which protrudes from beneath the butt.

These guns were often fired from a rest, or were provided with a slot through the fore-end stock through which a bipod or monopod could be inserted. This is a usual feature: modern Japanese rifles have been equipped with monopods. Otherwise the gun was held with the butt as a pistol grip to the right cheek, with the forefinger pressing the trigger. Nagasawa Shagetzuma, writing in 1612, shows galloping horsemen shooting at flying birds with these weapons.

Some multi-barrelled guns were built usually revolving in a pepperbox fashion. Pistols were made, but in design they are simply short versions of the longer arms. Examples a few inches long are found.

Japanese matchlocks are usually finely made, with lacquered stock and beautifully inlaid barrels.

Snapping matchlocks of the Japanese pattern were made in Indo-China, Malaya and Burma. These are cruder than the Japanese guns.

PR

WHEEL-LOCKS AND FLINTLOCKS

Wheel-locks and flintlocks are types of mechanisms in which sparks are generated by the friction of a mineral such as iron pyrites or flint against a steel surface. These sparks are directed into the priming pan of the gun, from which fire is communicated to the charge through the touch hole.

That fire could be produced by friction has been known since remote antiquity, and the origins of the wheel-lock are obscure. It is believed to have been invented in south central Europe late in the fifteenth century, though traditionally it has been ascribed to a Nuremberg gunsmith. A drawing by Leonardo da Vinci, dated circa 1508, shows two wheel-locks, but many of da Vinci's drawings show projected designs rather than devices which were actually constructed. A combined wheel-lock pistol and cross-bow in the Bavarian State Museum at Munich bears a coat of arms believed to have been in use during 1521–1526. The earliest dated gun believed to be genuine is a pistol of 1530 in the Royal Armoury at Madrid. These are developed weapons, and more primitive examples which are believed to be earlier cannot be exactly dated.

The mechanism is relatively complex (*see* 7). A steel arm known as a dog head holds a piece of iron pyrites, which at the time of firing is held above the priming pan of the barrel. A spanner is used to wind up a wheel against a spring; this wheel protrudes through the base of the priming pan. The priming pan has a cover, intended to stop the gunpowder from falling out or getting wet. When the trigger is pulled the pan cover is

Fig. 7 Action of a 17th century German wheel-lock rifle. The gun is in the firing position, with the pyrites lowered against the wheel

removed, and the dog head lowers the pyrites and presses it against the steel wheel, which rotates. The resulting sparks fire the gun. With some guns the priming pan has to be lifted manually. The majority are so arranged that the dog head faces the firer, but some are found upon which it faces away from him.

The wheel-lock mechanism enabled guns to be kept loaded and ready to fire, for the first time: one of the earliest documents relating to wheel-locks describes an accident. An additional advantage from the military point of view, was the absence of a glowing match which could reveal the presence of troops at night.

The invention of the wheel-lock made the pistol practical, and quantities of short, easily concealed guns were made. The effect on violent crime was considerable, and a quantity of rigid legislation which sought to control the use of wheel-lock guns in cities dates from the early sixteenth century.

The wheel-lock was complex and expensive to make, and never replaced the more simple matchlock entirely. Unlike the matchlock, it does not seem to have been produced outside Europe.

64

Throughout the sixteenth and seventeenth centuries, the wheel-lock was gradually replaced by snaphaunce and flintlock arms. These were more robust, less complex, and probably cheaper to produce. Guns may be found which have been converted from wheel-lock to snaphaunce or flintlock (*see* **8**).

A steel arm known as a dog, dog-head or cock, driven by a spring, strikes a piece of flint against an upright steel plate, known as the steel or frizzen. The resulting sparks are directed into the priming pan. Snaphaunce guns are those having the steel separate from the pan cover, and seem to be the earlier types. The flintlock proper has a combined pan cover and steel. The distinction is modern.

The origins of both types of lock are obscure. The snaphaunce seems to have been developed in the Low Countries during the first half of the sixteenth century.

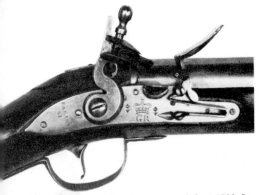

Fig. 8   The lock of an English flintlock gun of about 1730. It is in a loading position; the steel or frizzen is open to allow the pan to be primed with powder; the action is at half cock. The flint is firmly held with the leather patch

The true flintlock is believed to be the invention of Marin le Bourgeoys of Lisieux, Normandy, France. A gun signed by him in the Hermitage Museum at Leningrad probably dates from before 1610. Transitional types are known to have been made by his brother Jean, who died in 1615.

Another type of flintlock is known as the miquelet (*see* **9**). This seems to be a Spanish or Italian invention of the late sixteenth or early seventeenth century. This has a horizontally operating arm which crosses the lock-plate to act directly on the heel of the cock.

Flintlock arms remained in use in Europe until the first half of the nineteenth century, during which they were replaced by percussion lock arms. Flintlock guns were made throughout the world, usually with locks exported from Europe. The miquelet remained the most popular form in North Africa, Turkey, the Middle East and Ceylon. The flintlock was rarest in China and Japan, where the transition from matchlock to percussion was made quite briefly during the nineteenth century.

Fig. 9   A miquelet lock on an 18th century Arab gun. The external spring crossing the lockplate can be seen

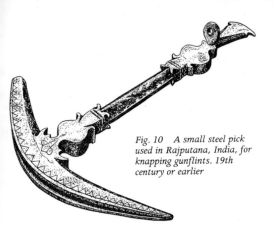

Fig. 10   A small steel pick used in Rajputana, India, for knapping gunflints. 19th century or earlier

Flintlock guns have been made during most of this century, initially for export to Africa and the Indies, and more recently for the use of European and American enthusiasts. Both the guns and their ammunition compete very favourably in price with sporting guns of more modern design.

Gunflints were initially prepared by striking chips or spalls from the surface of flint or chert nodules which are found naturally in many parts of Europe. A short pick was used. During the early eighteenth century the prehistoric technique of knapping long flint blades from the prepared cores of the nodules was rediscovered. The main English flint mines were at Brandon, Savenham, Tuddenham and Mindenhall. These were apparently re-opened late in the seventeenth century, and Brandon was worked until the present century. A flint of average quality lasts for some twenty to fifty shots.

Pocket Pistol

Overall lengths: 12–20 cm
Barrel lengths: 5–10 cm

The example shown is typical of the first quarter of the nineteenth century. It was made by J. & W. Richards of London. These short barrelled pistols were intended only for self-defence, and are inaccurate beyond a few yards. The smaller examples are often described as muff pistols.

To load, the barrel is unscrewed, revealing a breech of smaller calibre. This is charged with powder, a ball is rested upon it or in the barrel, and the barrel is screwed back on. The small square lug beneath the barrel enables it to be unscrewed with a tool resembling a spanner should it be too tight.

The square box-lock, the sliding safety catch at the base of the hammer, the folding trigger, and the slab sided walnut butt are typical features of these pistols.

This pistol is of .36 calibre, amongst the smallest usually encountered. Calibres normally range from .38 to .50.

Pistols of this type remained in use until the second quarter of the nineteenth century, when many were converted to percussion. The hammer replaced the jaws of the flintlock, the steel or frizzen was removed, and the sides of the priming pan cut down. The touch hole was bored to accommodate a nipple.

Percussion pistols of very much the same design were produced.

CMB

Pocket Pistol with Bayonet

Overall lengths: 15–20 cm
Barrel lengths: 8–15 cm

This typical pistol of the late-eighteenth or early-nineteenth century, was made by Thomas Archer of Birmingham. The design is typical of flintlock pocket pistols, and later percussion pistols, for the first half of the nineteenth century.

The bayonet is hinged from the screw-off barrel. The stud locking it in the extended position can be seen above the hinge. Pressing this stud enables it to be folded back along the side of the barrel, its tip being held by the catch on the right side of the box lock. When the bayonet is folded back, it is under tension from a leaf spring at its base, which is pressed against the barrel. Pulling back the trigger-like spur of the catch causes the bayonet to flick out and lock into position.

Hinged bayonets of this type first appeared in the seventeenth century, and became widespread in the second half of the eighteenth. They were a popular and useful addition to defensive weapons such as blunderbusses and pistols, since these were generally single shot weapons. Once the shot had been fired, the firer was helpless.

As the revolver replaced the single shot pistol, the bayonet almost disappeared as an addition to pistols. It is very occasionally found on European revolvers, the Dolne and the Delhaixhe being the best known examples.   CMB

Pistols

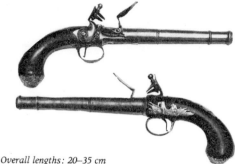

Overall lengths: 20–35 cm
Barrel lengths: 10–25 cm

The pair shown is by Robert Loy of London. Cannon-barrelled pistols of this type are often described as Queen Anne pistols, but in fact they were made during most of the eighteenth century. This pair was made about 1750.

A turned barrel resembling that of a cannon became popular during the second half of the seventeenth century, and is still found on box-lock pistols of the beginning of the nineteenth century. Some examples have rifled barrels.

To load, the barrel is unscrewed. This can usually be done by hand, but a small lug is usually provided at the beginning of the barrel, so that a spanner-like wrench can be used. The chamber has either a smaller bore than the barrel, or a constricted mouth. This is charged with powder, and the bullet placed upon the mouth, which is concave. In this way a ball can be used which is tight enough to engage the rifling, but which would be difficult to load from the muzzle.

The silver decoration of the butt is typical of good-quality eighteenth-century pistols. Smaller pistols of the same type are often found with silver wire inlaid into the butts.

The calibre of this example is .60, the normal range of calibres being .45 to .65.   QAB

Duelling or Target Pistol

Overall lengths: 30–40 cm
Barrel lengths: 22–26 cm

This typical late-eighteenth century pistol was made by Gillet of Bristol. These are frequently described as duelling pistols, but were doubtless more frequently used for target shooting. The practice of duelling with pistols seems to have arisen during the 1770s, as it was becoming unfashionable to wear a sword with everyday dress. Pistols intended for duelling generally have no shiny metal fittings or decoration which might catch the eye of the opponent. They are usually stocked to the muzzle, and have no butt or fore-end caps. Notch rear-sights and bead or small blade fore-sights always appear.

The wooden ramrod held by two brass pipes is usual, and was not replaced by all-metal swivel ramrods until the end of the flintlock period.

The octagonal barrel does appear on earlier pistols, but increased in popularity throughout the nineteenth century. It remains in use on a number of revolvers. Rifled barrels are sometimes found.

The calibre of this pistol is .65, amongst the largest normally found on this class of pistol. The normal range was .45 to .55.

CMB

Holster Pistol

Overall lengths: 30–40 cm
Barrel lengths: 20–25 cm

This is a typical military style pistol of the late eighteenth or early nineteenth century. Such pistols were carried by cavalrymen, travellers on horseback, and when equipped with a belt hook, by sailors. The holster was carried on the saddle rather than worn on the person. These pistols remained in use until replaced by very similar percussion pistols by the mid-nineteenth century.

No sights are provided; this is quite typical of such weapons, which were intended for use at close ranges. They were expected to be solid and reliable, and seldom show any unneeded decoration. Such pistols would have been the usual equipment of the highwayman. The calibre of this example is .70. Calibres of military and similar naval pistols varied between .56 and .75.

This one was made by Ketland and Company of London. The firm was based in Birmingham, and the majority of their arms were made there. The Ketlands were amongst the first Birmingham gunsmiths to compete with the London gunsmiths, during the 1760s. Amongst other Birmingham gunsmiths, they played some part in the establishment of a Proof House there. They proved their own barrels under Ordnance supervision whilst the Ordnance Proof House was being built, in 1796–97.

Two of the Ketland family emigrated to Philadelphia, Pennsylvania in 1789, and Ketland and Company locks are found on a number of American arms. QAB

Blunderbuss Pistol

Overall lengths: 40–80 cm
Barrel lengths: 25–40 cm

The blunderbuss, usually a short carbine or a pistol, was a defensive weapon intended to fire a heavy charge of large shot at close range. Such guns were popular for household defence, and were also suitable for guarding vehicles, prisoners and confined spaces such as gateways. They could be used in an offensive rôle when boarding ships, when no great range was needed.

The first examples appeared in Europe early in the seventeenth century, and continued in use until the mid-nineteenth century, when they were superseded by pepperbox revolvers, short carbines loaded with buckshot, and short shotguns.

The belling of the muzzle has no effect on the spread of the shot, but doubtless had some psychological effect on the people at whom it was pointed. Contrary to popular belief, these guns were not intended to fire nails or stones, which would have ruined the barrels.

Many weapons of this type have a flick-out bayonet mounted above the barrel. This folds along the surface of the barrel, and is retained by a catch which protects its tip.

The example shown is Turkish, and was probably made in Istanbul in about 1830.   SI

73

Wheel-lock Musket

Overall lengths: 110–150 cm
Barrel lengths: 60–100 cm

The example shown is a German smooth-bore muzzle loader made early in the seventeenth century. It is of .75 calibre. The absence of decoration suggests that this was a military weapon. Such guns were made largely in Germany and Holland. Presumably they were made for elite troops, since they were very much more expensive and more liable to malfunction than the common matchlock.

The pistol-grip, trigger-guard and raised cheek piece on the butt assist in aiming. Bead fore-sights and notch rear-sights are provided. Many examples are rifled.

The action of the example shown is in the firing position. The wheel, covered by the circular plate, is wound up or spanned, by a spanner which fits the square axle which can be seen protruding from the circular plate. The cock is lowered, and holds the pyrites against the wheel. When the trigger is pulled the wheel spins, striking sparks from the pyrites into the gunpowder in the priming pan. Fire is passed through the touch-hole into the breech of the gun.

Imported weapons of this type were used in England during the Civil War, alongside the common matchlock. **PR**

Dog-Lock Musket

Overall lengths: 150–155 cm
Barrel lengths: 112–117 cm

The weapon illustrated is a standard English military musket of circa 1688.

The point of interest is the dog-lock. This is a catch which can be seen behind the cock or dog of the lock, which engages a notch in it when it is raised. This enables the weapon to be carried ready to fire, but safe.

The dog-lock seems to have been introduced on flintlock and snaphaunce weapons early in the seventeenth century, and had generally disappeared from English military weapons by the beginning of the eighteenth century. It was superseded by the half-cock position which became normal on the developed flintlock. Occasional weapons are found which have both a half-cock position and a dog-lock. Probably some customers preferred a safety mechanism which they could see to one which they could not.

When inferior steels are used, or when arms are in a worn or dirty condition, there is no question that the dog-lock is infinitely safer than the half-cock. For this reason some nations retained it on their military arms until the mid-nineteenth century, and it is commonly found on private weapons, in particular pistols, until the end of the muzzle-loading era. Its major military usage seems to have been between 1620 and 1720.   SI

Combined Musket and Grenade-launcher

Overall lengths: 150–155 cm
Barrel lengths: 112–117 cm

In the third quarter of the seventeenth century there was an increased interest in the grenade as a weapon. The grenade was normally thrown by hand, but attempts were made to devise launchers. In 1681 Thomas Swain and John Tinker were both rewarded for their efforts in this field. Thomas Swain's device was unsuccessful, but John Tinker's weapon was taken into service, and is known as Tinker's Mortar. An example is illustrated.

The butt of the gun opens to reveal a mortar or launcher. The priming pan of the lock communicates both with the breech of the musket barrel and, through a tube, with the breech of the mortar in the butt. Priming powder is poured into the tube through a slot behind the cock. A flat plate in the rear wall of the pan is raised to allow fire to pass into the tube. A rest is folded under the fore-end stock: this and the muzzle of the musket barrel rest on the ground when the gun is being used as a mortar.

When the gun is in use as a normal musket, it is improbable that the mortar portion could safely be left loaded.

Normal grenade-launching muskets were fitted with a discharger cap at the muzzle. This system, with adaptations, has remained in use.

The weapon illustrated was made by James Peddell of London, circa 1685.   SI

Musket

Overall length (average): 160 cm
Barrel length (average): 115 cm

The example illustrated is a typical English military musket of the second quarter of the eighteenth century. It was made by William Wooldridge of London in 1722.

These weapons are known as pre-Land Pattern. They are the earliest of the large class of musket generally known as the Brown Bess. They are of .75 calibre.

The rather Dutch style of the late seventeenth century English musket is combined with more modern features taken from French muskets and from contemporary sporting guns.

During this period the parts of the locks become less flat and angular, and gradually more rounded. The dog-lock disappears, as the half-cock becomes more relied upon. The butt-plate, trigger-guard, ramrod-pipes and other furniture become more usually of brass than of iron. Like the lock parts, the furniture becomes more rounded, and is progressively more inlet. Barrel bands disappear, to be replaced with pins which engage loops in the bottom of the barrel. This makes it difficult to get the barrels off these guns, but the soldier was not supposed to do this.

There is no rear-sight, and the fore-sight also does duty as a stud which locks onto the socket bayonet which came into general use.

Except in stylistic detail, these weapons hardly changed until the nineteenth century.

SI

Double-Barrelled Rifle and Musket

Overall lengths: 120–130 cm
Barrel lengths: 80–90 cm

This is an Austrian sporting gun of about 1725. One barrel is rifled and the other is smooth-bore, the barrels being placed one above the other.

The right hand lock and front trigger fire the upper, smooth-bore, barrel and the left hand lock and back trigger fire the lower, rifled barrel.

Bead or blade fore-sights and notched folding rear-sights are provided. The pistol-grip trigger guard is typical.

The ramrod is commonly mounted on the right side, between the barrels, as on this example.

Weapons of this type were not unusual in Austria and Germany, where a powerful and versatile weapon was sometimes needed in case of boar and bear. Combined rifles and shotguns are still made, usually consisting of a double-barrelled shotgun, with a rifle barrel below and between the shotgun barrels.

Rifle

Overall lengths: 100–200 cm
Barrel lengths: 60–150 cm

This is a Turkish weapon of the late seventeenth or early eighteenth century. Heavy rifles of this design were produced from the sixteenth to nineteenth centuries. The shape of the stock is typical, and became popular throughout Turkey, Persia and Northern India.

Earlier weapons were matchlocks. The miquelet lock, clearly visible on this example, became popular in the mid-seventeenth century, and was made until the mid-nineteenth century, when it was supplanted by the percussion lock. Many weapons were converted from miquelet to percussion. Good barrels were treasured, and nineteenth century percussion weapons with European style stocks may be found with seventeenth-century barrels.

Weapons of large calibre, such as 1 in., are encountered. Some of these are excessively heavy and must usually have been fired from a support.

Button triggers are not uncommon, but have often been replaced with European style triggers. Trigger guards were generally added at the same time.

Ramrods were not always provided: often they were carried separately.   SI

Boat Gun

Overall lengths: 75–100 cm
Barrel lengths: 50–75 cm

The piece shown is a specialized type of long-barrelled blunderbuss, formerly used by naval, coastguard and customs personnel. The intention is to scatter a heavy charge of large shot at close range, when boarding a ship, when repelling boarders on a ship, and when firing in the dark at ill-seen targets.

Most such weapons have brass barrels, since brass was believed to have more resistance to corrosion, especially salt water induced corrosion, than gun metal. The belling of the muzzle, which is quite usual, has no effect whatever upon the pattern of the shot, but does enable the gun to be loaded more easily in a rocking boat.

Most surviving boat guns have flintlock ignition, and are of eighteenth or early-nineteenth century manufacture. Many were mounted upon swivels. Usual calibres were 4 to 2 bore.

The boat gun seems to have become obsolete when the first effective repeating pistols, pepperboxes and then revolvers, came into use.

The example shown is a 2 bore by R. Farlow of London, made in about 1730.   PR

Rifle

Overall length (specimens vary): 124 cm
Barrel length (specimens vary): 86 cm

The example shown is a breech loader made by the London gunsmith Durs Egg in 1774. The design was patented by the Huguenot refugee Isaac de la Chaumette in London in 1721, and improved upon by his compatriot Bidet. During the remainder of the eighteenth century, the design was used occasionally for sporting guns. Marshal Maurice de Saxe (1696–1750) advocated its military use in carbines, but it seems that none were made. Captain Patrick Ferguson, then of the 70th Regiment, improved the design during the 1770s, to reduce the effects of fouling. The arm was demonstrated before George III in 1776, and Ferguson was granted a patent in that year, to prevent the design falling into other hands.

Arms of the type illustrated have come to be known as Ferguson rifles. In 1777 a Corps of Riflemen was set up, from elements of the 6th and 14th Regiments, and commanded by Ferguson. The Corps sailed for America in 1777, and the Ferguson rifle saw action in the American War of Independence. Thus it seems to have been the first rifle used by a British force.

A rotation of the trigger guard unscrews a plug vertically through the breech of the barrel, allowing ball and powder to be placed in the chamber through the resulting aperture in the top of the barrel. The breech is shown open. The chamber is of a larger calibre than the bore, so that the ball is forced to engage the rifling. The barrel is of .68 calibre, and the rifling is eight groove.   SI

81

Volley Gun

Overall length: 94 cm
Barrel length: 51 cm

A number of weapons of this type were made by the London gunsmith Henry Nock from 1779 onwards. A private designer, James Wilson, claimed to have invented the weapon, which was accepted by the Board of Ordnance as possibly of use 'on board ships to fire from the round tops'.

The guns were initially tested at Woolwich, and underwent sea trials off Portsmouth, on board HMS *Phoenix*. It appears that their first active service was with Admiral Howe's fleet at the Siege of Gibraltar in 1782.

There are seven barrels, muzzle-loaded, of 32 bore. One barrel is central, the others being in a circle around it. The action fires only the central barrel, holes being bored through to communicate fire to the chambers of the outer barrels. Some weapons were rifled, but the majority were smooth-bore.

A number of naval commanders, Nelson in particular, objected to weapons being fired from the tops of their ships, because of the risk of setting sails on fire.

Guns of this type saw brief sporting popularity. One double gun, a fourteen barrelled monstrosity, was made by W. W. Dupe of Oxford. This is inscribed 'Perdition to conspirators' and 'With this alone I'll defend Robro Camp. 1795'.   SI

Spear Carbine

Overall lengths: 115–135 cm
Barrel lengths: 76–96.5 cm

During the 1780s the British military authorities continued to try to develop a satisfactory breech-loading flintlock weapon, since the Ferguson rifle had not proved satisfactory.

The London gunsmith Durs Egg was approached by the Duke of Richmond, Master General of the Ordnance, to make two carbines in which the regulation paper cartridges could be used. The first two were made in 1784, one being presented to George III and the other being retained by the Ordnance Office. A weapon of this type is illustrated.

The breech, which is shown open, is hinged at the rear, and is loaded from the front. The long spear bayonet, when not in use, is fitted onto the gun in reverse, so that its tip rests in a clip in front of the trigger-guard. Some weapons were made with rifled barrels, and some smooth-bore.

In 1786 a quantity of these weapons were issued to the Light Dragoons on an experimental basis. They reported their findings in 1788, but the Duke of Richmond had lost interest in them.

The locks of these guns are of interest. They appear to be conventional flintlocks, but are in fact screwless, clips and spigots being used. These were designed by Jonathan Hennem of Lewisham in 1784.

The breech-loading mechanism of this type was designed first by Giuseppe Crespi in Milan, and was tested by the Austrian cavalry in the 1770s. It was abandoned because of excessive gas loss. Urbanus Sartoris of London patented an improved arm of the same type in 1817, and yet another in 1819.

Rifle

Overall length: 116 cm
Barrel length: 76 cm

The example illustrated was the first rifled weapon to be accepted for service in the British Army in any significant quantity. It is a muzzle loader of .625 calibre, designed by the London gunsmith Ezekiel Baker.

The Baker rifle was in production from 1800 to 1838, and was rendered obsolescent by Lovell's improved Brunswick rifle, in 1837. This was a percussion weapon.

The design derives ultimately from the German Jäger rifle of the late-seventeenth century. The rifling is seven grooved, making a quarter twist in the barrel length. The brass pistol-grip trigger-guard, and the cheek-piece on the butt, assist in aiming.

To engage the rifling when fired, the ball had to be hammered into the gun, especially if the bore was foul from previous shots. This could meal the powder and distort the bullet, making the arm less accurate. It was slow to load and fire. An alternative was to wrap the ball in a cloth patch, which was greased or moistened with saliva.

The Baker rifle was the first type of weapon to be set up at the present Royal Small Arms Factory at Enfield Lock.   PR

Wall Piece

Overall lengths: 175–215 cm
Barrel lengths: 135–190 cm
Weight: 10–55 kg (20–120 lb)

Outsize muskets of this type were made throughout the eighteenth century. The example shown was made about 1790. As their name implies, their role was semi-static and defensive.

The calibre of the English pieces is supposedly .89, or $6\frac{3}{4}$ bore. French examples tend to be about .75 calibre.

General Lallemand, writing during the Napoleonic Wars, gives the range of the 2 bore as 900 metres at 4 degrees elevation, and the 10 to 14 bores a point-blank range of 140 metres.

Rifled guns of this type were made during the American War of Independence. Colonel Fielding Lewis proposed a rifled 4 bore to defend rivers against warships, and to begin battles. A number of rifled 4 bores and 8 bores were made at Rappahannock Forge in Virginia.

Weapons of the type shown, but better made to private order, were popular amongst Georgian wildfowlers as punt-guns. They were lashed into the bows of a punt, and loaded with large shot. A double punt-gun with one flintlock and one percussion lock, brought down 14,000 wildfowl to the Georgian sportsman Peter Hawker. The object of using both types of lock was to give a more extended string of shot, since the flintlock is slower than the percussion to fire.

Modern punt guns, whose bore cannot legally exceed 1.75 in. are generally loaded through a screw-in breech plug. A .32 centre-fire revolver blank fires the black powder cartridge, which is hand loaded. Some percussion muzzle-loaders are probably still in use.   SI

Musket

Overall length: 58.5 in.
Barrel length: 42 in.
Calibre: .75 in.

The weapon illustrated is a New Land Pattern musket of about 1803. This type of Brown Bess was introduced in the middle of the Napoleonic Wars, shortly after the signing of the Peace of Amiens (1802). The object was to return to peace-time levels of manufacture and inspection, to modernize the military musket, and to make it on something like a production line basis. There were brief periods of manufacture in 1802–1803 and 1814, but production could not begin in earnest until after the war ended, in 1815.

The stocks of these muskets are simplified, presumably to do away with unneeded detail and speed up manufacture. The comb of the butt loses its rail, and the carving around the breech and the lock disappears. Perhaps the only mechanical improvement is that the ramrod is slightly swollen towards its end, and its channel somewhat widened, so that it is less likely to fall out. Browning of the barrels was introduced in 1815.

At the end of the flintlock period vast quantities of these muskets were in store. They were not generally converted into percussion arms, since it cost as much to make new percussion arms. Many were purchased by private firms for export.   SI

Indian Rifle

Overall lengths: 110–200 cm
Barrel lengths: 70–150 cm

The flintlock was introduced to India by the various European nations who set up trading posts around the coast and who subsequently colonized the interior. By the beginning of the nineteenth century the flintlock was sufficiently well known and available to allow Indian gunsmiths to produce flintlock guns in quantity. The locks were normally imported from England, and bear the markings of the East India Company: the example shown has an East India Company lock.

The fore-sight is a bead, and the rear-sight a pierced block 'peep' sight. The barrel is rifled. Rifled barrels are found on a number of Indian matchlocks and flintlocks, but the smooth-bore seems to have been more usual.

Whilst Indian flintlocks are not uncommon, they never entirely replaced the cheaper and simpler matchlock.   SI

PERCUSSION GUNS

The mechanical action of a percussion firearm is generally similar to that of a flintlock, but is somewhat less complex. It differs in depending for its ignition upon a group of explosives known as fulminates, which explode when struck.

A number of chemists working in the seventeenth and eighteenth centuries discovered the properties of various fulminates. Attempts were often made to adapt them for use in firearms, by themselves, as additives to gunpowder, and as a substitute for saltpetre in gunpowder. Due to the extreme sensitivity, instability, and extreme power of the fulminates, the attempts were not successful.

Attempts were made to use fulminates as the priming powder in the pans of sporting shotguns, because it was often found that the flash of the flintlock startled game birds. The delay between the flash of the flintlock and the firing of the shot was sufficient for wary birds to remove themselves from the line of fire. Though quick and smokeless, fulminates did not make reliable priming powders.

The first efficient percussion lock was designed by the Reverend Alexander John Forsyth, of Belhevie, Aberdeenshire. This consisted of a bottle-shaped magazine and detonator which pivoted on a pierced plug which ran into the touch-hole of the breech of the gun. The pierced plug had a chamber in it, above which was a spring-mounted firing pin, seated in the upper part of the bottle. The lower part of the bottle contained sufficient fulminate for about twenty-five shots. The bottle was rotated to allow a charge of fulminate to

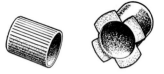

Fig. 11   Percussion caps: the larger cap, with the flanges, is meant for muskets, the flanges allowing its easy removal after firing. The smaller cap is for a pistol. Both types are still made

enter the chamber in the pierced plug. When returned to the upright position, the magazine was cut off from the chamber by the wall of the plug, and the firing pin was aligned with the hammer of the gun. When the hammer fell, it drove the pin against the powder in the chamber, detonating it. Fire then passed down the centre of the plug into the breech of the gun.

Forsyth seems to have made the first of these locks in 1805, and to have used it on a sporting gun for a season. In 1806 he was appointed to superintend production for military use, based on his design, but he soon fell into disfavour. In 1807 Forsyth patented his invention, and in 1811 established a Patent Gun Manufactory in Piccadilly.

Other, usually simpler, systems of percussion ignition were rapidly invented. The end product was the percussion cap, a simple pressed copper cup containing fulminate. This is still made, and is the ancestor of the primer in the modern centre-fire cartridge. It was placed over a nipple communicating with the breech of the gun, and fired by the blow of the hammer upon it. This was invented in about 1815–1820, but by whom is not known. A number of gunsmiths claimed to have invented it. The first patent was to Prélat of Paris in 1820.

The most important effects of the percussion system were on the manufacture of pistols. For the first time repeating pistols could be made efficiently, and the revolver became common. Most of the features of the modern revolver evolved during the percussion period.

Percussion arms were generally superseded by cartridge arms by the third quarter of the nineteenth century: it was the invention of the percussion cap that made the cartridge possible. But many percussion arms are still in use, and they have never ceased to be made.

Percussion arms have probably been made in most parts of the world. They are most seldom encountered in the Far East, where the transition from matchlock to cartridge was brief.

Fig. 12   An alternative percussion system: this carbine action was intended for Maynard tape primers. The magazine for the primers is shown with its lid open; it held a paper roll of caps, similar to those still used in toy pistols

Pocket Pistol

Overall lengths: 15–20 cm
Barrel lengths: 5–15 cm

This typical mid-nineteenth century pistol was made by G. Price of Bristol. The type derives from flintlock pistols, and examples may be found which have been converted from flintlock. These pistols remained in use until cartridge breech loaders became commonplace.

The square box-lock, the sliding safety catch engaging the base of the hammer, and the slab sided butt are usual features of these pistols. Folding triggers are often encountered.

To load, the barrel is unscrewed. If it is tight, a wrench resembling a spanner is used. This engages the square lug seen beneath the barrel. The breech, of smaller bore than the barrel is charged with powder, and the ball is rested upon it or placed in the barrel, which is then screwed back on.

Examples of this type with very short barrels are known as muff pistols. The calibre of this one is .45: normal calibres ranging from .38 to .60. Pistols of the larger calibres are sometimes known as man-stoppers.

Outside Europe, pistols of this type were made in America, India, and Japan. The Japanese examples usually have pleasantly engraved brass frames, and are finely made. Pistols of a similar type have been made in Europe recently. They generally have rather rounded white-metal frames, and rounded butts with plastic grips. Spur triggers are found. Engraving is unusual. They are normally of .38 calibre. QAB

Belt Pistol

Overall lengths: 15–20 cm
Barrel lengths: 8–10 cm

Pistols of this type were produced throughout England and Ireland in the mid-nineteenth century. The example shown is by George Gibbs of Bristol. Generally they are of a size convenient for the overcoat pocket, and have a long flat hook on the left side of the stock, by which they can be hung from the belt. Swivel ramrods are usual.

Most such pistols have back-action locks, as has the example shown. Most have a bead fore-sight, and a groove along the top of the barrel. The groove type of sight became commonplace during this period, and has remained. It can be found on many modern pocket automatic pistols.

The barrels are seldom rifled. The example shown is of .50 calibre, which is common. Calibres vary between .38 and .60, pistols with the larger calibres being known as man-stoppers.

These pistols were often made without a belt hook, and without it are described as coat-pocket pistols.

All these pistols were made for self-defence at close ranges, and are generally incapable of accurate fire beyond ten yards, in common with many modern pocket automatic pistols. CMB

Military Pistol

Overall lengths: 15 in. (military), 11.5 in. (naval)
Barrel lengths: 9 in. (military), 6 in. (naval)

The pistol shown was made at the Tower of London in 1852. The design was introduced by George Lovell in 1842, and pistols of this type remained in use until replaced by revolvers.

The swivel ramrod, absence of sights, and butt-plate, often equipped with a loop for a lanyard, are typical of military, naval and police pistols of this period. The naval or coast guard models are fitted with belt hooks.

Minor varieties of these pistols are numerous, since many of them were made up from older flintlock parts. The calibres vary from .753 (cavalry), .567 (naval) to .653 (East India Company).

Pistols seem to have been unpopular with the military authorities of this period, and little effort was put into their development. At times it was stated to be 'an ineffectual weapon' and 'worse than useless'. It was abolished as a cavalry weapon in 1838, though the Lancers were allowed to keep theirs. Subsequently each cavalry regiment was issued with thirteen pistols, for sergeant majors and trumpeters. The weapon shown is one of this type.

During this period the percussion revolver was being developed, and seems to have been accepted with enthusiasm by many officers, who purchased their own.   CMB

Target or Duelling Pistols

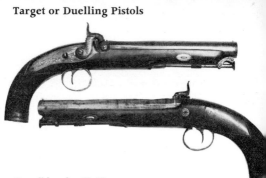

Overall lengths: 25–38 cm
Barrel lengths: 23–26 cm

This matched pair of pistols was made by James Purdey of Oxford Street, London, probably during the 1840s. Though often described as duelling pistols, they are in fact simply good quality large pistols of which many gentlemen had a pair, and were doubtless more often used for target practice than for any other purpose.

In England the practice of duelling declined as percussion pistols became widespread, except, apparently, amongst army officers. In 1844 an amendment to the Articles of War put an end to this. The last recorded duel in the British Army took place in 1843.

The back-action side-locks of these pistols appeared during the early 1830s, and had become common by 1850. The advantage is that the weight of the lock lies more naturally in the wrist of the stock, lightening the fore-end. The sliding safety catch, engaging the base of the hammer, is usually found on pistols of this quality. Swivel ramrods are quite usual.

This pair of pistols has traps in the butt plates, under which percussion caps could be kept.

The barrels have notch rear-sights and bead fore-sights; this is typical. The calibre is .57, which is common, but one of the larger calibres found on pistols of this type.   CMF

94

Two-Barrelled Pistol

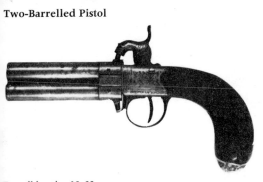

Overall lengths: 12–22 cm
Barrel lengths: 7–14 cm

This is a typical English coat-pocket pistol of the mid-nineteenth century. It is of respectable quality, but has no maker's marks. The barrels are of .36 calibre.

The barrels are rotated by hand to bring them into firing position beneath the hammer. They are held in place by a strong internal spring. The curved steel plate in front of the trigger guard stops the percussion cap of the unfired barrel from falling off.

The eight deep grooves in the muzzle of each barrel, often mistaken for rifling, are intended to allow a key to be used to unscrew the barrels for cleaning. The barrels are made separately, only being connected at the breech. Pepperbox pistols with this system of barrelling are also found: they are usually Belgian.

This type of pistol remained popular until the smaller pocket revolvers became popular. Being smaller, cheaper and flatter than the revolver, they were ideal personal defence weapons. They are not capable of accurate fire, since the hammer obscures the target.

Flintlock pistols of this type are found, but less commonly, as they were rather more complex to build. Most two-barrelled pocket pistols of this type were probably produced during the period 1830–1860. MABA

Two-Barrelled Pistol

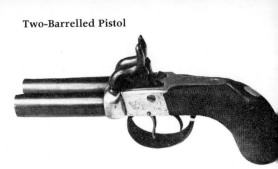

Overall lengths: 18–23 cm
Barrel lengths: 9–12 cm

This English pocket pistol of the mid-nineteenth century has two side-by-side barrels and a brass frame. Though the gun is of good quality, there are no maker's marks. It is of .45 calibre.

Each hammer has a separate lock. Unusually, the front trigger serves the left barrel and the rear trigger the right: this is a reversal of the usual layout. The barrels are not connected with one another other than by being screwed into the same breechblock.

Pistols with side-by-side barrels are not particularly common in England, over-and-under being the more usual layout. Pistols of this construction are comparatively wide, and make rather bulky pocket pistols, though they are probably more robust than many over-and-under pistols, and can be fired more quickly than those whose barrels were rotated by hand.

The side-by-side pistol lasted into the pin-fire period, and was popular in Europe. Larger holster pistols of the type are found.

The absence of maker's marks on pistols of this period is not significant. It simply suggests that the gunsmith felt that the additional work of adding his name would not add to his sales of pistols. It suggests either a busy city gunsmith making run-of-the-mill pistols, or a country gunsmith without significant competition.

QA1

Overall lengths: 18–25 cm
Barrel lengths: 10–15 cm

This English pistol was made in about 1850. It has six barrels of .38 calibre, which rotate as the trigger is pulled.

The percussion pepperbox was the first widely used multi-shot pistol. Most European manufacturers of the period 1830–1860 made pepperbox pistols. Breech loading cartridge pepperboxes were made after this period, the American pistols of James Reid being the best known.

The example shown is quite typical. Some have a vertical slit in the body of the hammer, to assist aiming, this being the only common type of sight. Some have belt hooks, and some have daggers attached to them, the latter provision being rare. Commonly there are five to six barrels, but specimens with from three to twenty-four barrels are known.

This type of weapon seems to have appeared in the mid-sixteenth century, but until the invention of the percussion cap could not be made safe or convenient, and so was uncommon. The earliest nineteenth-century pepperboxes did not have automatically turning barrels; this had to be done manually. Perhaps in the 1830s the principle of automatic rotation was rediscovered. It had been used earlier, for instance by John Dafte of London (1640–1680), but when or by whom it was discovered is not known.

These weapons are the parents of the true revolver. The first revolvers were basically short pepperboxes with a barrel added.

PR

97

Underhammer Pepperbox Pistol

Overall lengths: 18–25 cm
Barrel lengths: 10–15 cm

This pistol was made by James Rock Cooper of Birmingham circa 1845. It has six barrels of .30 calibre.

The hammer is in the butt beneath the axle of the barrel and strikes the nipples as the trigger is pulled. The trigger rotates the barrels.

This streamlined type of pepperbox was perhaps the best. Eye injuries from flying pieces of metal from the percussion caps did occur: the layout of this weapon minimized such a risk. The gun can be taken out of the pocket and aimed more quickly: having the hammer exposed over the barrel obstructs both activities. The construction is more simple than that of the normal pepperbox pistol. It cannot easily be fired by accident, as the hammer is internal and cannot be knocked against the percussion cap. The conventional pepperbox can fire if dropped, used as a club, or even in the pocket if the hammer is struck.

These weapons remained in use well into the revolver period, being cheaper, often more robust, and quicker to load. They are certainly safer to the user, as one barrel cannot easily communicate fire to the next, and the consequences would not be serious if it did.

As the barrels rotate until the moment of firing, accurate shooting is difficult. No sights are provided.

These pistols became obsolete as the revolver developed into a more accurate and more powerful weapon.

Transitional Revolver

Overall lengths: 26–35 cm
Barrel lengths: 13–18 cm

This mid-nineteenth century pistol is mechanically the earliest effective type of revolver. This example is English, but has no maker's marks, and may be either an experimental weapon or a cheap revolver.

The type is known as transitional, since it has obvious features of the pepperbox, and obvious features of the revolver as we know it.

This example has six chambers and is of .40 calibre. The butt and action are clearly parts which could equally well have been used for making a pepperbox, and perhaps were originally parts of one. The cylinder is basically a short pepperbox barrel assembly. The barrel is smooth-bore, and the screw securing it to the stock is the axle of the cylinder. A fore-sight is provided, but as it is obscured by the hammer not much use can be made of it unless one has a strong grip and fires quickly.

Later transitional revolvers have nipples which fire directly into the chamber, and a less obtrusive hammer which strikes towards the back of the chamber rather than the top. Barrels were later rifled, though very cheap revolvers with smooth bore barrels are found even in this century.

The revolver seems to have been invented in the sixteenth-century, and examples with matchlock and flintlock ignition are found. However, the principle only became safe enough for general use when the percussion cap was invented, and not really safe until the advent of the metallic cartridge.   PR

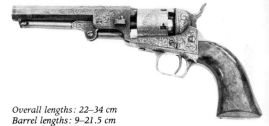

Overall lengths: 22–34 cm
Barrel lengths: 9–21.5 cm

The first truly successful percussion revolvers were designed by Samuel Colt of Hartford, Connecticut, and were patented in England in 1835, and in the United States in 1836. Prototypes were produced by Anson Chase of Hartford, and John Pearson of Baltimore. The Colt Patent Arms Manufacturing Company started at Paterson, New Jersey, in 1836. The Colt revolvers were the first to be produced on a factory basis.

The patent describes how a chamber of the five-shot cylinder was locked in alignment with the barrel when the hammer was cocked. The patent survived contests until expiry in 1857.

The Colt revolvers were single action only: the hammer has to be cocked manually before each shot. Though pepperboxes are double action, Robert and John Adams of London patented a double-action revolver in 1851, and purchased a patent granted to Frederick Beaumont, of Barnsley, Yorkshire, which enabled them to make revolvers capable of double or single action.

Single-action fire is claimed to be more accurate, but the double-action revolver or the pepperbox is very much quicker. So long as the revolver was regarded for use at close quarters in an emergency, the single action was held in disfavour.

Colt pocket revolvers were made in calibres .28, .31, .34 and .36. Police and naval revolvers were made in .36 calibre. The military revolvers are in .44 calibre.

Colt revolvers have been copied since they were first produced, and copies are still being made in Italy.   PR

Sidehammer Revolver

Overall lengths: 26–35 cm
Barrel lengths: 13–18 cm

The example shown is a .45 six-shot revolver, probably of English manufacture, made circa 1855. It has certain characteristics of the earlier pepperbox revolvers. The nipples are set vertically, and the hammer falls downwards onto them, from the left. The hammer does not interfere with the line of sight, and a notch rear-sight is provided: this can be seen mounted on the barrel.

A disadvantage of this type of weapon is that, because the nipple does not pass directly into the chamber, it is difficult to clean, and prone to fouling.

The example shown has deep ten-groove rifling.

Such revolvers were mostly produced in the mid-1850s. Though elegant and probably accurate, they did not obtain widespread use. QAB

Revolver

Overall length: 27 cm
Barrel length: 12.5 cm

A typical English revolver of the 1850s is shown. It is one of the earlier types of revolvers to be relatively successful.

The type is known as the Webley–Bentley. It was patented by the London gunsmith John Bentley in 1852, but patent rights were sold to Philip Webley of Birmingham in 1853.

The example illustrated has no maker's name. It appears that during 1853–60 these revolvers were sold to gunsmiths or other retailers, who applied their own names to the barrels.

The importance of Bentley's patent was that it featured a half-stop on the hammer, to hold it clear of the percussion cap when it is carried loaded. A triangular flange of metal in front of the rear-sight protects the shooter's eyes from flying pieces of percussion cap, as these revolvers are open frame.

Loading is from the front of the chambers on the right side of the gun. Percussion caps are placed on the nipples as they are rotated past the right side of the gun. The rammer on the left side of the barrel is used to tamp down each charge as the cylinder is rotated past the rammer head.

The example shown is of .45 calibre and has five-groove rifling. It is capable only of double-action fire. Raising the hammer completely obscured the rear-sight.

Some revolvers of this type have flick-out bayonets on the side of the barrel.

Pocket Revolver

Overall length (pocket pistols): 22 cm
Barrel length (pocket pistols): 11.5 cm

This is a typical, good-quality, English pocket revolver of the third quarter of the nineteenth century. The design is by the Birmingham gunsmith William Tranter, and the gun was made by J. Venables of Oxford.

To load, the axle is pulled out from the front, allowing the cylinder to be taken out. The cylinder, which has five chambers of .32 calibre, is loaded with gunpowder and ball. The copper percussion caps are then placed on the nipples of the chambers, having first been squeezed slightly so that they cannot fall off. The cylinder and axle are then returned. A rammer can be seen laid along the left of the barrel; this is raised above the barrel, and the charge is tamped down in each chamber as the cylinder is rotated past the rammer head.

The revolver can be fired by single or double action: Tranter patented this mechanism in 1856. The fixed rammer or loading lever was patented in 1855.

Tranter's earlier revolvers, patented in 1853, had two triggers, one for cocking the hammer, and one for firing or double action.

Heavier weapons of the same design, up to .45 calibre, were made for military and naval use. A model for dragoons had a detachable carbine stock.   PR

Grapeshot Revolver

Overall lengths: 25–30 cm
Barrel lengths: 12–15 cm

Arms of this type were patented by Francois Alexandre Le Mat, of New Orleans, Louisiana, in 1856 and 1859. They are commonly known as Le Mat revolvers.

Percussion, pin-fire and centre-fire examples are found. Most were made in France, as was the one illustrated, but some are believed to have been made in England and the United States. Their first military use seems to have been during the American Civil War. One model was issued to the French Navy.

The lower barrel does duty as the axle of the cylinder, and is thus central. The lower barrel is generally shorter than the upper, of a larger calibre, and smooth-bored. A shot cartridge was fired from it.

A prototype revolver of this type was made by John Krider of Philadelphia in 1859.

Revolving rifles on this principle were invented by James Miller, of Brighton, New York, in 1829. The best known makers were William Billinghurst, of Rochester, New York, and Benjamin Bigelow, of Marysville, California. Billinghurst had worked for Miller as a gunsmith, and may have set up his own business when Miller went into the wholesale fish trade. Bigelow was an apprentice of Billinghurst before moving to California.

SI

Walking-stick Gun

Overall length: 109–117 cm (with stock)
*   86–94 cm (without stock)*
Barrel length: 66–74 cm

These are disguised weapons made for a variety of purposes from the mid-eighteenth to the late-nineteenth centuries.

The example shown is of a type patented by John Day, of Barnstaple, Devon, in 1823. It is an underhammer percussion muzzle-loader of .50 calibre. Many such weapons were fitted with detachable shoulder stock, normally carried in the coat pocket. The example shown has the stock fitted.

These underhammer guns are of very simple construction. The action has only three parts, mainspring, trigger and hammer. When not in use the hammer lies against the barrel, and the trigger fits into a slot. Cocking the hammer raises the trigger. The action is shown in the cocked position. A ramrod is carried inside the barrel, and a ferrule protects the muzzle and keeps in the ramrod. This example has a bead fore-sight.

Walking stick guns are generally made entirely of steel, except for the wooden shoulder stock, and sometimes parts of the handle. Sometimes the metal barrel was treated or overlaid to appear wooden.

These guns were intended for self-defence and for the use of game-keepers. Doubtless many were also used by poachers. There are rare flintlock examples, but the flintlock mechanism is too bulky to be easily concealed in this way.

A strange flintlock weapon of this type was patented by van de Kleft in 1814. It contained a flintlock pistol, a telescope, pen, pencil, paper, a knife, an inkwell, a screwdriver and various drawing implements.   CMB

105

Police Carbine

Overall lengths: 42.5 in., 37 in. (Indian)
Barrel lengths: 25.5 in., 21 in. (Indian)

Police weapons of this type were common in the mid-nineteenth century. They are smooth-bore muzzle loaders of .656 calibre, intended to fire ball or buckshot.

The example shown is an experimental model of circa 1840. It differs from the normal 1840 model in having no fore-sight, and in having a fixed flick-out bayonet. At this time some thought was given to the possibility of assailants' taking a policeman's bayonet away from him: thus, presumably, this fixed bayonet. Other models are equipped with a socket bayonet which has a spring catch to stop its being snatched from its scabbard.

Except for the Indian Native Police Carbine of the 1856 model, police weapons do not generally have any rear-sight.

The design of this weapon derives originally from percussion conversions of the Paget Cavalry Carbine of 1808.

From the 1860s, police carbines were produced from military models of .577 calibre, converted to centre-fire breech-loaders by the Snider system. A buckshot cartridge for these was approved in 1868, and issued to prisons. It was thought to be non-lethal beyond about 75 metres. The buckshot was of 220 bore.

The Indian Native Police Carbine has been made again in large quantities, initially from old parts, but now from entirely new parts. These are intended for wall decorations or to deceive collectors, and cannot safely be fired.

PR

Naval Rifle

Overall lengths: 45.75–46.25 in. (army),
48.75 in. (navy)
Barrel lengths: 30 in. (army),
32.5 in. (navy)

The example shown is a Brunswick Heavy Navy Rifle made at the Royal Small Arms Factory, Enfield Lock in 1840. It is of .796 calibre, the normal Brunswick rifle being of .704 calibre, and took a heavier charge of powder. The type was developed for use in the fighting tops of ships. Sea trials were carried out from HMS *Excellent*.

The first Brunswick rifles were approved in 1837, to replace the flintlock Baker rifles then in service. They were the first percussion rifles issued to the British Army, and remained in use until gradually replaced by the 1842 and 1853 pattern rifled muskets. The naval model was still in use in the 1860s.

This type of rifle was apparently developed by a Captain Berners, Field Adjutant to the Duke of Brunswick, and was submitted to the military authorities by a Mr Seabright, acting for the Duke.

The rifling consists of two wide rounded grooves making one complete turn in the length of the barrel. A special bullet was designed for this rifling, consisting of a spherical ball with a raised belt around it. The raised belt engaged both grooves of the rifling. Some difficulties were encounted in placing the belted ball in exactly the right position on the muzzle for loading, especially, one assumes, in action. A normal spherical ball, of smaller size, in a greased linen patch, also performed well and was more quickly loaded. The patch engaged the rifling.   SI

Repeating Rifle

Overall lengths: 120–130 cm
Barrel lengths: 70–80 cm

This repeating rifle was invented by Lewis Jennings of Windsor, Vermont, USA, and was patented in December 1849.

Ignition is by means of a percussion cap or fulminate pill. The tubular magazine, which can be seen below the barrel, is loaded with hollow-based bullets containing their own propellant charges of gunpowder. These were the invention of the New York cartridge-maker George Arrowsmith, and were patented in England in December 1847. The ring trigger also serves as a lever, allowing bullets to be fed from the magazine to the breech of the gun.

This lever-operated tubular magazine may be considered the ancestor of those designed by Tyler Henry and by the Winchester Repeating Arms Company, of New Haven, Connecticut.

Surviving Jennings rifles are found as single shot weapons, suggesting that the gravity-feed tubular magazines did not stand up to hard use.   SI

Revolving Rifle

Overall lengths: 98–140 cm
Barrel lengths: 53–94 cm

The first truly successful revolving rifles were designed by Samuel Colt, of Hartford, Connecticut, and built at his Paterson factory in New Jersey. The eight-shot Paterson rifle first saw military service in 1838, in the Seminole Indian War.

The weapon illustrated is an 1855 model six shot .44 calibre rifle, made in London. Such weapons are rare, as the Colt Patent Firearms Manufacturing Company only operated in London between 1853 and 1857. Other such rifles were made at Hartford, Connecticut. A number of other revolving rifles were made by United States gunsmiths, and revolving shot-guns were also made. The system was not adopted with any enthusiasm outside the United States, and became obsolete as the metallic cartridge was adopted. Revolving rifles saw their greatest military use during the American Civil War.

Powder and ball are loaded from the front of the cylinders below the axle. Percussion caps are placed on the nipples as they pass to the right of the hammer. A rammer can be seen beneath the entry of the barrel: this is pulled down to tamp down the charges in each chamber as they pass below the axle.

The tangent rear-sight is shown in the raised position.

In action, if clumsily loaded and dirty, a revolving rifle can be a most dangerous thing. The ball is slowed by fouling in the barrel, left from previous shots, and the flashback can be communicated to other chambers, firing them when they are not in alignment with the barrel. If this happens, the firer may well lose his left hand or arm.   PR

Carbine

Overall length: c. 94 cm
Barrel length: c. 50 cm

During the late 1850s the British Army accepted three breech loading percussion arms for experimental cavalry use. These were designed by Christian Sharps, Calisher & Terry, and William Green.

The example illustrated is the rarest of these by the London gunsmith William Green, made in 1856. It never obtained a footing as recognized service arm.

The type of ignition is of particular interest. It has a mechanical priming system containing a roll of caps, very similar to those in use in modern toy pistols. In the illustration the cap box is open. The strip of caps extrudes from the action behind the nipple, being projected over it one by one. When the hammer strikes them the flash is communicated to the chamber through the nipple.

This system of priming was patented by the well-known Washington dentist Edward Maynard in 1845. Maynard ignition was used on some Jenks, Sharps and Symmes carbines and on some revolvers. The revolvers are probably the rarest weapons built on this system.

Weapons with Maynard priming probably saw their only military use during the American Civil War. They were soon superseded by metallic-cartridge breech-loaders.

Double-Barrelled Carbine

Overall length (average): 107 cm
Barrel length (average): 66 cm

In 1820 Lord Charles Somerset suggested that a carbine be designed for a cavalry unit at the Cape of Good Hope. This idea was rejected by the Duke of Wellington, but accepted the next year. The weapons were made at the Royal Small Arms Factory, Enfield Lock, under George Lovell and Jonathan Bellis.

The first issue of these was in flintlock. All such guns were subsequently made with percussion locks. They were issued until about 1854. The example shown was made in 1845.

The later weapons were rifled, either when made or later, with four broad grooves. A number were made by private manufacturers, and it is now hard to distinguish regulation arms from those made to private order.

A similar type of carbine, but with a bar for a sword bayonet on the outside of the right barrel, was approved for use by Irish police in 1839. These were designed by the Birmingham gunsmiths Tipping & Lawden.

A further type was developed by Major John Jacob, the commander of the Sind Irregular Horse, about 1856. He also designed a pointed 32 bore bullet, having four raised belts to engage the rifling. One of his last inventions was a bullet containing a charge of explosive, with a percussion cap in its nose, which exploded on impact.

The Cape carbines obtained sporting vogue in South Africa. One barrel could be loaded with ball, and the other with shot.   SI

Japanese Snapping Percussion Gun

Overall length, (average): 125 cm
Barrel length, (average): 95 cm

The weapon illustrated is a .75 calibre smooth-bore muzzle loader. These were produced during the third quarter of the nineteenth century, often by converting matchlock weapons; as early European percussion weapons are conversions of flintlocks. Apart from Anglo-Indian guns, these are the only Oriental percussion weapons. They are rare, as the transitional period from matchlock to breech loading cartridge weapons was brief in Japan.

The mechanism of the example shown is basically that of the sixteenth century European snapping matchlock. The hammer is cocked against the spring seen on the outside of the lockplate. The button trigger which releases this can be seen protruding from the butt beneath the tail of the lockplate.

In this instance the fore-end stock is pierced to allow the gun to be fired from a bipod. PR

EARLY CARTRIDGE GUNS

As a container for a single charge, the cartridge has been known for some five hundred years. The earliest cartridge was simply a charge of gunpowder wrapped in paper; it gave its name to thick paper now known as cartridge-paper. This was torn open for loading into the muzzle of the gun. By the end of the sixteenth century it had become customary to attach the bullet to the cartridge, or to include it in it.

A number of early shotgun cartridges contain only the shot and wads. The object was simply to have a ready-measured load. This was sometimes in a wire cage, to hold the shot in a tight pattern.

The cartridge as we now know it is not simply a container for the propellant charge and the bullet. It contains its own means of ignition, an explosive known as a fulminate, which detonates and fires the cartridge when its percussion cap or rim is crushed by the hammer or firing pin of the gun. When the cartridge fires, it expands to seal the breech of the gun so that propellant gases generated by the explosion of the charge cannot escape. The cartridge is thus an essential part of the breech of the gun.

The invention of the breech-sealing cartridge made breech loading weapons practical for the first time. Breech loading guns are known to have been used at the beginning of the fifteenth century, and it is quite possible that there were breech loading guns earlier than that. Breech loading forms of guns with matchlocks, wheel-locks, flintlocks and percussion ignition are all known, but all lose varying amounts of gas at the breech.

During the nineteenth century numerous inventors sought, with varying degrees of success, to produce cartridges having the two essential characteristics, of breech-sealing, and of containing their own ignition. This had not been done previously, as it depended upon the knowledge that fulminates explode when struck, and that this explosion can be used to fire a charge of gunpowder. This knowledge had given rise to the percussion system of ignition.

Examination of British, French and American patents alone show many hundreds of cartridges. Precisely who invented what detail of each type cannot be known, as patentees may often have pirated or bought ideas from less worldly inventors, and as the best cartridges were a combination of various ideas.

The first centre-fire cartridge was patented by Jean Samuel Pauly of Geneva in 1812. This had a brass case with a nipple in the centre of its base. On the nipple was seated a fulminate pill or a percussion cap. A similar shotgun cartridge was made, having a brass base and a rolled paper body. Centre-fire cartridges were developed throughout the nineteenth century. The nipple gradually gave way to a cavity containing an anvil. The percussion cap, which came to be known as the primer, was seated firmly in the cavity in the base of the cartridge. The hammer or firing pin of the gun drove the primer against the anvil, exploding the fulminate, and firing the cartridge through vents in the bottom of the cavity. Small cartridges of this type could be pressed out of sheet copper, but larger cartridges had to be made of card, like modern shotgun cartridges, or from spirally wound brass sheet, until deep-drawing techniques were developed at the end of the nineteenth century. Pauly's cartridge was the ancestor of most modern ammunition.

The pin-fire cartridge was patented by Lefaucheux of Paris in 1835, and improved by Houiller in 1846. The

114

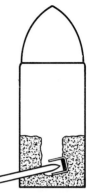

Fig. 13   Pinfire cartridge

percussion cap lies on its side in the base of the cartridge, held in place by wires or a card wad. A pin, with its tip inside the percussion cap, protrudes through the side of the base of the cartridge. The hammer of the gun falls upon the pin, which is driven against the fulminate. This explodes and fires the cartridge. The pin-fire cartridge was extremely popular, and was the first to attain world-wide use. Lefaucheux's invention of this cartridge enabled him to produce the first practical double-barrelled breech-loading shotgun, the ancestor of most modern sporting shotguns. The pin-fire cartridge is now obsolete: only reloadable brass shotgun cartridges of this type are now made.

The needle-fire cartridge was invented by Johann Nikolaus von Dreyse, of Sömmerda, Prussia. He had previously worked with Pauly. The fulminate was seated in the base of the bullet, which was mounted on a card tube containing the charge of gunpowder. The action of the gun drove a needle through the gunpowder to strike the fulminate. The earliest cartridges of this type were for a muzzle-loading gun designed by von Dreyse and his partner Collenbusch in the late 1820s. By 1841 a breech-loading gun for these cartridges was produced by von Dreyse alone. This was a bolt-action weapon, the ancestor of the modern bolt-action rifle. Though popular, the system was not truly effective, as the card cartridge could not properly seal the breech of the gun.

The rim-fire cartridge was originally simply a percussion cap with a bullet seated in it. The explosion of the fulminate propels the bullet: there is no charge of powder. Such a cartridge was patented in England by John Hanson and William Golden in 1841, and in France by Flobert in 1849. Ammunition of this type was usually intended for target practice at short ranges, and was suitable for indoor amusement. The cartridges are still made, and are known as Flobert.

The rim-fire cartridge was improved by B. Tyler Henry and others, working for Smith and Wesson of Springfield, Massachusetts. Their cartridge had a more pronounced rim than the Flobert, and the fulminate was inside the fold of the rim rather than evenly spread all over the inside of the base. They also contained a

Fig. 14   Cartridges: a) rimless centre-fire; b) rimmed centre-fire; c) rim-fire

propellant charge. Smith and Wesson did not patent this until 1860, though they were producing revolvers to fire it in 1857. This was the ancestor of the modern rim-fire cartridge, which in .22 calibre is the most widely used civilian rifle and pistol cartridge.

A number of inventors produced self-consuming cartridges of paper, gold-beaters' skin, collodion and other combustible materials. The possibility of self-consuming cartridges, which do not need extraction or ejection, is still periodically investigated. Inexact machining, and fouling from the combustion of the powders and case materials then in use, made the self-consuming cartridge impractical during the nineteenth century.

As the invention of pin-fire and centre-fire cartridges enabled the breech-loading shotgun to be developed, the practice of choke-boring barrels became general. Choke is a constriction towards the muzzle of a gun, varying in shotguns from 3 to 40 thousandths of an inch. The effect of this constriction on a pattern of shot is very considerable. A fully choked barrel will place 75 per cent of a charge of shot in a 30 inch circle at 40 yards, whereas a cylindrical barrel will only place 40 per cent of the same charge in the same circle at the same range.

Choke-bored rifles were also produced, generally with the intent of making a versatile sporting weapon, suitable for use with bullet or shot. The idea was resurrected before and during the Second World War, to give increased muzzle velocity and penetration to anti-tank rifles and some types of light artillery.

When or by whom the technique of choking was invented is not known. It was presumably a jealously guarded trade secret of a gunsmith specializing in sporting guns.

Deringer Pistol

Overall lengths, original types: 10–23 cm
Barrel lengths, original types: 4–10 cm
Calibres: .22–.51

This is perhaps the best-known type of small pocket pistol, in use from the 1830s to the 1930s. Some of the cartridge models have been made again recently in the United States, in .22 and .41 calibres, rim fire.

The original pistols produced by Henry Deringer of Philadelphia (1786–1868), were compact single-barrelled percussion muzzle-loaders with rifled barrels and back action sidelocks. Pistols of this type have been made recently, for instance at Eibar, Spain.

The first cartridge model, in .41 rim-fire, was patented by Daniel Moore in 1861. The favourite cartridge model, the double-barrelled type shown, was produced until 1935, and again has been produced recently for collectors. The example shown has English proof-marks, and was imported into England in quantity.

The superimposed barrels tip upwards to load when the lever above the spur trigger is depressed. They are hinged at the top of the breechblock. The same firing-pin strikes alternately the top of the bottom chamber and the base of the top chamber.

Somewhat similar four-barrelled pistols were produced by Christian Sharps of Philadelphia.

These pocket pistols are now obsolete, having been superseded by small automatics. They were favourite murder weapons, one of them being used for the assassination of Abraham Lincoln.

Handbag Pistol

Overall lengths: 10–12 cm
Barrel lengths: 4–5 cm

During the second half of the nineteenth century revolvers of this type gradually replaced short percussion single shot pistols as defensive weapons for women. These are generally chambered for 5 mm pin-fire or 6 mm rim-fire ammunition. The design is basically the same whichever type of ammunition was used, only varying in the breech of the chambers and the shape of the hammerhead. These pistols seldom exceed 15 cm in length.

The example shown is a six shot 6 mm rim-fire revolver. Loading is through a port to the right of the hammer. The swing-out ramrod beneath the barrel is used to push the empty cartridge case out as the chambers are rotated past the loading port. This is a typical arrangement. Folding triggers are usual.

This pistol is of good quality. It is inlaid with gold and silver and has ivory grips. A velvet lined leather case was provided. Unusually, there are no maker's marks or proof marks, but such pistols are usually Belgian or French.

Such weapons have become obsolete. Their place was taken by small automatic pistols of .22 or .32 calibre, and tear-gas pistols of 6 mm or 8 mm calibre.

CMB

Pocket Revolver

Barrel lengths: 2.5, 3, 3.5, 4, 5, 6, 8, 10 in.

The pistol shown was made by Smith & Wesson of Springfield, Massachusetts, between 1868 and 1875. It derives from a .22 calibre revolver introduced in 1857.

This is a five-shot single-action revolver taking a .32 calibre rim-fire cartridge. A latch at the front base of the frame is unlocked to allow the barrel to fold upwards. The cylinder can then be slid off its axle for loading. Empty cartridges are removed by pushing the rammer bar fixed beneath the barrel through each chamber of the cylinder. The hammer has no half cock for safety. The spur trigger is typical of this series of pistols.

The weapon shown has had part of the spur of its hammer removed. This damage is sometimes found on Victorian pocket pistols, also on double-barrelled carbines. It seems that the hammer combs sometimes caught on things.

Many thousands of these pistols were produced. They were extremely popular and have remained not uncommon. At the turn of the century a Smith & Wesson official is reported to have said that their .32 calibre pistols had killed more people in the previous twenty or thirty years than all the pistols of all their competitors.

CMB

Pin-Fire Revolver

Overall lengths: 12–40 cm
Barrel lengths: 3–20 cm

This is a typical revolver of the third quarter of the nineteenth century, and was produced in such quantities that it remains one of the commonest types of antique firearm.

Loading is effected through the port behind the cylinder on the right: this can be seen in the illustration. Ejecting spent cases is done through the loading port by pushing back the ramrod beneath the barrel. This is mounted to the right of the cylinder axle, in a tube with a retaining spring. This pistol has six cylinders taking 9 mm pine-fire cartridges. Generally they have five or six cylinders for 9 mm or 7 mm cartridges: 5 mm and 12 mm weapons were also made; these are somewhat less common. The barrel is rifled: smooth-bore pin-fire revolvers are rare.

The example shown is French or Belgian, circa 1860. It is described as the naval model, since the engravings on the cylinder are copied from Samuel Colt's Old Model Navy Pistol of 1850. The majority of the weapons seen now are Belgian.

These are the earliest effective cartridge revolvers, and were first produced in quantity in France. It used the first widely used breech-loading cartridge, patented by Lefaucheux in 1835, improved by his son Eugène Lefaucheux, and by Houiller in 1846. The type of revolver which uses this ammunition is widely known as Lefaucheux. More than a million such revolvers were produced, largely in Belgium, France and Spain.   PR

Palm Pistol

The model illustrated is the Protector revolver, apparently invented by Jacques Turbiaux of Paris. It is typical of the squeezer pistols made largely in France, Belgium and the USA during the last two decades of the nineteenth century. These pistols are not held and fired in the normal fashion, but are grasped in the palm of the hand, with the barrel protruding between the first and second fingers, and fired by tightening the fist. They are therefore not capable of being aimed with any accuracy, but were intended only for self-defence at close quarters. The squeezing action fires the pistol by forcing the cylinder to revolve, which cocks and drops the firing pin against the rim of the cartridge as it comes into alignment with the barrel. The cartridges are loaded by unscrewing one of the sideplates and placing them in a turret-like cylinder.

The European pistols seem to have used a 6 mm or 8 mm rim-fire cartridge, and the American pistols a .32 rim-fire cartridge. The majority of them seem to have been in the larger calibre, and to have been capable of seven shots. Some of the French pistols in the earlier calibre were capable of ten shots.

These pistols were easy to conceal, being no larger than the larger of the cheap pocket watches of their day. All are now rare, and seldom found in working order.

P

Gaulois Pistol

This was one of the most popular of the late nineteenth-century French squeezer pistols, and perhaps the best designed and most robust. It can be aimed, as the barrel rests on the forefinger, but is really intended for self-defence at close quarters. The action of squeezing it makes it awkward to aim.

Its operation is unusual. The front of the grip, containing the magazine, rests against the fingers. Clenching the fist removes the top cartridge from the magazine, inserts it into the chamber, and fires it. Releasing it, which one naturally does upon the recoil of the cartridge, ejects the spent cartridge case. The resemblance to an automatic pistol is superficial, the force of recoil not being used in any way. It has a slight advantage over an automatic pistol, as a defective cartridge will not hinder it, but will be ejected normally when manual pressure is released.

The better Gaulois are attractively engraved, and come in what appears to be a good leather cigar case. Part of the bottom of the cigar case, below the slot which houses the pistol barrel, is a receptacle for additional cartridges. The pistol is capable of five shots, and most seem to have taken an 8 mm centre-fire cartridge. It is only 15 mm thick, and very easily concealed.

PR

Knuckleduster Pepperbox

This type of double weapon was patented by James Reid of New York in 1865, and is known as 'My Friend'. As a knuckleduster, or rather, club, the pistol is held muzzle upward in the hand, butt outward, with the little finger through the loophole in the butt. There are five-shot examples of .32 calibre, and, less commonly, seven-shot examples of .22 calibre. Perhaps all take rim-fire cartridges.

This pistol has a simple but unusual type of safety catch. This has to be strong, as when the pistol is used as a club, the cylinder must be locked so that the cartridges are not aligned with the hammer, otherwise it could fire if a blow was struck with it, as the heel of the hand may press upon the hammer. The safety catch protrudes from the frame of the pistol in front of the trigger. This is connected to a bar, at the end of which a stud engages whichever barrel is aligned to it. This can only be done when the hammer is between two cartridges in the cylinder. Thus these pistols have an uneven number of chambers.

Barrelled versions of this pistol were also produced. These are all-metal revolvers with the Reid butt and safety catch.

PR

Multi-barrelled pistols of this type were popular in Europe and America during the period 1860–1920. Being only 2–15 mm thick they could easily be concealed in the clothing. The concept is now obsolete, since modern pocket automatic pistols can fulfil the same role.

The example illustrated is Belgian, of 5 mm calibre, circa 1875. The trigger is folded forward; as it is pulled back the firing pin moves from chamber to chamber. The barrels are hinged at the front of the frame, and fold forward for loading and the removal of spent cartridge cases. There is a very similar French pistol, with four barrels of .22 calibre.

Pistols of this type seem to have been invented by William Marston of New York, and patented in 1857. The first was a three-barrelled percussion muzzle-loader. Cartridge pistols were later produced in .22 and .32 calibres. Some were equipped with short sliding daggers, and an indicator showing the number of chambers fired.

A more modern type is the Reform pistol, in .25 calibre. Here there are four barrels fixed to a rising block, the firing-pin remaining in one position. Pulling the trigger raises the barrel assembly, fires the aligned chamber, and allows gas to escape into the previously fired chamber to eject the spent cartridge case from it.

PR

Two-Barrelled Revolver

Overall lengths: 20–30 cm
Barrel lengths: 10–15 cm

This French twenty-shot revolver was made in about 187
There are many similar revolvers, mostly Belgian and Frenc
having 16, 18 or 20 shots, of pin-fire, rim-fire or centre-fi
ammunition.

The example shown takes 6.35 mm centre-fire cartridge
An extremely similar type, probably by the same maker, tak
16 .32 centre-fire cartridges.

The chambers in the cylinder are arranged in tw
concentric circles. The hammer has two strikers, but th
chambers are so spaced that only one cartridge is fired at
time, chambers of each circle being fired alternately. Th
frame is hinged at the top and opens upwards for loading. Th
empty cartridges are removed simultaneously by pushing th
ejector-rod beneath the barrels.

An American percussion revolver by Aaron Vaughan
Pennsylvania has both barrels bored in the same block, th
right higher than the left. It also has two hammers of differer
shapes, to fall on nipples in different rows, operated by th
same trigger.

Four-Barrelled Pistol

Overall lengths: 15–35 cm
Barrel lengths: 10–20 cm

These pistols were made by Charles Lancaster & Co. of New Bond Street, London. The example shown is circa 1889. Large pistols of this type were used by big game hunters, who needed something tough and reliable. These are both, when compared to some of the rather delicate heavy revolvers of their day. Lancaster also made four-barrelled rifles. Braendlin of Birmingham also made four-barrelled and some six-barrelled pistols in the 1890s.

Smaller four-barrelled pistols with Deringer-type spur triggers were made by Christian Sharps of Philadelphia from the 1850s to the 1870s. These were in .22 or .32 calibre. Similar pistols in .22 calibre were produced in Europe recently.

Generally the barrels are hinged to the base of the breech, unlock at the top, and fold downwards for loading. Some slide forwards to load. The firing-pin is mounted on a circular plate, and rotates as the trigger is pulled.

At first sight the Lancaster pistols appear to be smooth-bore, but in fact have a twisted oval bore. Lancaster was the best known exponent of the oval-bore system of rifling, but it is not known who invented it or when. The Russian Johan George Leutmann advocated it in 1735.

Pistols of the Lancaster, Braendlin and Sharps type became obsolete as the revolver was bettered. They were barrel-heavy, and clumsy, particularly in the larger calibres—the Lancaster fired a special .476 cartridge. A complaint about the Braendlin was that the shock of the recoil was sometimes sufficient to fire another chamber—this suggests over-sensitive cartridges rather than a faulty gun. PR

Saloon Pistol

Overall lengths: 28–38 cm
Barrel lengths: 20–30 cm

Long-barrelled breech-loading pistols of this type, intended only for indoor target practice, were made during the second half of the nineteenth century, mainly in Europe. This example was made by George Gibbs of Bristol.

The trigger-like arm in front of the trigger guard is pulled back to unlock the barrel, allowing it to hinge forward for loading and unloading. The spur on the trigger guard is a platform for the second finger, to assist in aiming.

The hammer alone, held by the mainspring, is sufficient to hold down and fire the cartridge, which was quite weak and had little recoil. There is generally no breech-block on these weapons. When there is, it usually consists of a hinged block with a slot through which the hammer can strike the cartridge.

These pistols are generally of 6 mm or .22 calibre, though 4 mm and 9 mm pieces are sometimes encountered. The ammunition was of Flobert type, and contained no propellant charge. The detonation of the priming composition alone gave the bullet sufficient power. The ammunition is still made. *The use of any other type of ammunition in these pistols is most dangerous.*

CM

erhaps two dozen different penknife and pistol combinations
ere produced in Europe and the USA between 1860 and
930. These weapons were intended for self defence. An
merican advertisement of 1923 suggests that these weapons
ave a thousand uses, and illustrates a man shooting at an
normous dog which is about to bite a girl.

Raising the hammer of these pistols causes the trigger to
ick out, like the folding trigger of the contemporary pocket
istols. A cartridge can then be placed in the chamber, and the
istol fired. The hammer is substantial, and is designed to act
s the breech. Few pistols of this type could safely be carried
•aded.

The pistol illustrated was made by Unwin & Rodgers, of
heffield, England. This was one of the most popular and best-
iade types. This example is chambered for the .297 rim-fire
artridge, but the majority of penknife pistols took the .22
hort rim-fire cartridge. Examples taking pin-fire cartridges
re known, and seem to be of German manufacture. A few
ouble-barrelled Unwin & Rodgers pistols are known, but
iese are heavy and clumsy, and cannot have been popular.

There are muzzle-loading percussion examples of English
nd American manufacture. The Unwin & Rodgers percussion
istol is equipped with a ramrod and bullet mould. These can
e carried with it, as their handles are sprung, and they fit into
ots in the knife.   PR

Double-Barrelled Pin-Fire Shotgun

Overall lengths: 115–180 cm
Barrel lengths: 50–90 cm

The first effective breech-loading shotgu[ns]
were patented by Lefaucheux of Paris in 183[ ].
The example shown is a 12 bore of the 1860[ ]
by the London gunsmiths Robert & Jo[hn]
Adams.

To open the breech for loading, the lev[er]
beneath the trigger guard is swung to one sid[e,]
allowing the barrels to hinge downwards. [In]
many cases, the fore-end stock (removed [on]
the weapon illustrated), contains the lever. [A]
notch at the rear of each chamber allows th[e]
pin of the pin-fire cartridge to protrude abov[e]
the barrels of the gun: the hammers fall upo[n]
these pins to fire the cartridges.

It is usual for the front trigger to fire t[he]
right-hand barrel, and for the back trigger [to]
fire the left-hand barrel, but examples a[re]
found upon which one trigger, in differe[nt]
positions, fires first the right barrel and the[n]
the left.

These guns may be found in a variety [of]
calibres, from 4 bore to 32 bore. The cartridg[es]
were generally of paper, with brass heads, b[ut]
reloadable pin-fire cartridges of brass are sti[ll]
made, in 12 bore.

The centre-fire weapons of the 1860s ren[ ]
dered the pin-fire shotguns obsolescent. Mos[t]
disappeared when smokeless powders cam[e]
into general use. Few now survive in use, in th[e]
hands of enthusiasts. They may be regarded [as]
the immediate ancestors of the present doubl[e]
barrelled shotguns.

Garden Gun

Overall lengths: 90–105 cm
Barrel lengths: 46–60 cm

These are small-bore shotguns intended for killing vermin, and for crop protection.

Production commenced on a large scale during the third quarter of the nineteenth century, largely in Belgium. Most were sold in Western Europe. They were formerly popular in Britain, but legislation relating to the minimum length of shotgun barrels has put most of them out of use.

The example shown is Belgian, circa 1900. The action is the Flobert–Warnant rising block. To load, the hammer is cocked, permitting the breech-block to be lifted and swung forward over the barrel, to which it is hinged. This exposes the breech. The breech-block is then returned. The firing-pin passes obliquely through the breech-block. The hammer strikes the base of the firing pin, driving it against the rim of the cartridge. Extraction of the empty cartridge is automatic, a horse-shoe shaped extractor being pushed back as the breech-block is raised for reloading. This is a most simple, sturdy and reliable system, but is only suitable for low-powered ammunition. It is probably the oldest and most primitive system of breech-loading in use. More modern garden guns, usually German, French and English, have bolt actions. Some have box-magazines.

The normal calibre of these guns is 9 mm, but weapons of 5 mm, 6 mm, 7 mm and 8 mm are encountered. Only 6 mm and 9 mm ammunition is now made.

Rifle

Overall length: 130 cm
Barrel length: 80 cm

This type of single-shot bolt action rifle was invented by Johann Nikolaus von Dreyse, of Sömmerda, Prussia, in 1838. It was accepted for service in the Prussian Army in 1842.

These weapons are the ancestors of the modern bolt-action rifle. The bolt handle which can be seen on the right of the action, is lifted to the upright position, and used to pull back the bolt, exposing the breech. The cardboard cartridge is inserted, and pushed into the breech by the return of the bolt. The action of working the bolt cocks within it a long needle against a spiral spring. When the trigger is pulled, the needle is driven forwards through the gunpowder in the base of the cartridge, to fire a detonating compound placed in the base of the wad behind the bullet, which is enclosed in paper.

These rifles first saw extensive action in the Prusso–Danish War of 1864 and in the Seven Weeks War of 1866.

The drawback of this system is that the firing needle remains in the centre of the charge when it explodes. The needles became foul and corroded, and were often broken, so that soldiers had to carry a supply of them. The most serious objection is that the cartridge, being of paper, does not properly close the breech, and after some use the gas escape at the breech was such that the soldier was obliged to fire from the hip.

Needle-fire shotguns and revolvers, the latter very rare, were also made, some by the inventor's son Franz von Dreyse.

Muzzle-loading needle-fire guns were invented by von Dreyse, circa 1828.   PI

Rook Rifle

Overall lengths: 90–100 cm
Barrel lengths: 45–60 cm

English light sporting rifles of the late-nineteenth century are commonly known as rook rifles. At that time rooks were regarded as a pest, and some people made rook pie.

The rifle shown is a single shot 70 bore by Griffin and Worsley of Manchester. It is a rare type, being needle-fire. Most are centre-fire, metal-cartridge weapons, of calibres between .22 and .38. Most have Martini or Snider actions.

To load this weapon, the lever fixed to the right side of the breech is operated, to allow the barrel to fold down forward, exposing the breech. The hammer drives the needle into the cartridge.

These weapons were usually extremely well made, and were relatively expensive. As with garden guns of the period, barrels were often octagonal.

Until the advent of the mass-produced .22 rifle, these weapons were the only light sporting rifles used in England. The cheaper .22 sporting rifle, with its greater range and accuracy, rendered these weapons obsolete. Apart from those made for .22 rim-fire ammunition, they can no longer be used, as the ammunition has long been out of production. In recent years some have been bored out or had their barrels sleeved for use as .410 shotguns.   PR

Carbine

Overall lengths: 105–140 cm, depending on original arm converted
Barrel lengths: 60–100 cm, depending on original arm converted

A carbine made at the Royal Small Arms Factory at Enfield Lock is shown. This example is dated 1861, but was probably made in the later 1860s from Pattern 1861 Short Rifle parts. The design was submitted by Jacob Snider of New York in response to a British advertisement of 1864, which invited propositions for the conversion of muzzle-loading Enfield rifles into breech-loading weapons.

Arms converted by the Snider system were the first metal-cartridge breech loaders generally issued to the British Army.

About two inches of the barrel were cut out at the breech. A new breech, in front of this slot, was enlarged for the admission of a cartridge, initially of papier-maché and later of coiled brass. A breechblock, hinged at the right, fitted into the slot. A firing-pin passes obliquely through the breechblock. This is struck by the hammer shown at half-cock in the illustration. Extraction of the empty cartridge is by rotating the breechblock to the right and pulling it back along its hinge. The calibre is .577.

The Snider system was cheap and robust, and proved popular. Snider-type shotguns, usually 12 bore, and sporting rifles of .45 and .50 calibre, are found.

The Snider military arms became obsolete in the 1870s, as the Martini–Henry arms came into use. Some Snider rifles remain in civilian use, with the rifling bored out, as 20 bore shotguns.

PR

Rifle

Overall lengths: 116–124 cm
Barrel lengths: 75–85 cm

The Martini–Henry was the first metal cartridge breech-loading arm to be built as such for the British Army. It was adopted in 1871 as a replacement for the Snider arms, which were converted muzzle-loaders, or made up from muzzle-loader parts.

The breech mechanism was designed by the Austrian Friedrich von Martini, and the barrel by the Scottish gunsmith Alexander Henry. The calibre was .45, and the cartridge was the first bottle-neck type adopted by the British Army.

The breechblock, operated by the lever behind the trigger-guard, is hinged upon a pin at the rear. When the lever is depressed, the block falls, the firing-pin within it is cocked, the empty cartridge case is ejected, and the breech exposed for loading. Returning the lever allows the block to rise, and the rifle is ready for use. The example illustrated has an experimental quick loading device, consisting of a magazine to the right of the action. This flicks cartridges onto the loading platform which is the top of the block.

The Martini–Henry became obsolescent in the 1890s, as bolt-action rifles came into use. Large numbers were converted to .303 calibre; some of these still remain in civilian use. The spread of small-bore (.22) rifle clubs at the beginning of the twentieth century caused many to be converted to .22 calibre: some are still to be found in rifle clubs. More recently, a number of the original .45 rifles have been bored out as 20 bore shotguns.

The Martini action is still used for heavy .22 target rifles, especially in England.   PR

Double-Barrelled Rifle

Overall lengths: 90–100 cm
Barrel lengths: 45–60 cm

The example shown is a .30 calibre double-barrelled rifle by Holland and Holland of London, made late in the nineteenth century.

The action is much that of a shotgun. The lever between the hammers is pressed to one side, to release locks holding the barrels to the breech. The barrel assembly then tips forward for loading. An aperture sight, which folds down against the butt, can be seen in the raised position.

Double-sporting rifles have been made by the better English gunsmiths since the mid-nineteenth century. Usually the barrels are side by side, and are of the same calibre. Weapons with twin barrels of the same calibre over and under are rare.

These rifles originate in part from similar military weapons of the period 1839–1853, used in Ireland, India and South Africa, and in part from double-barrelled shotguns.

They have remained popular, though always expensive, since in theory a sporting weapon, unless it is automatic, cannot fire a second shot as quickly. It is probable that these rifles are used mainly by sportsmen whose normal weapon is the shotgun. These rifles suit the shotgun user, as the balance and action is essentially the same as that of the shotgun. PR

MODERN CARTRIDGE GUNS

The design of firearms has always been basically dependent on the capabilities of the explosives in use as propellants. The crude and improperly mixed gunpowders of the Middle Ages were used in crude and unreliable weapons. The preparation of consistently reliable gunpowders, late in the matchlock period, enabled reliable weapons to be built.

As we have seen, the cartridge containing its own means of ignition was developed during the nineteenth century. Until such cartridges were devised, successful repeating arms could not be built. Towards the end of the nineteenth century smokeless gunpowders, or nitro powders of the modern type came into general use. In their early days these powders varied considerably in their performance, from manufacturer to manufacturer, and even from batch to batch. At the same time, until the perfection of modern deep-drawing techniques, cartridges of reasonably consistent dimensions and strengths could not be produced.

Until cartridges of almost identical performance could be mass produced, reliable self-loading and automatic weapons could not be developed. Such weapons depend for their action either upon the recoil of their firing, or upon the gases generated by the explosion of the charge in the cartridge. In either instance, the cartridges must be manufactured to very close tolerances.

In terms of effective range, accuracy, and reliability, the development of the cartridge has enabled firearms design to progress further in the last hundred years than in the previous six hundred years. The 4.85 mm automatic rifle currently being developed at the Royal Small Arms Factory, Enfield Lock, is as different from the bolt-action rifles of both World Wars as they were different from the single shot breech-loaders of the 1870s. But the muzzle-loading military musket of the 1850s, hardly differed from that of the 1650s, save in its means of ignition.

Weapons are now being improved every few years, usually in terms of lightness, rate of fire, and versatility. Progress in the electronic and optical fields during the last few years has resulted in the production of extremely sophisticated sighting equipment.

Within the next few decades, it seems probable that some completely new types of firearm will be developed. One direction in which this may take place lies in the perfection of the self-consuming cartridge, or of the bullet containing its own means of propulsion. Such a development would completely alter the construction of self-loading and automatic weapons. A step in this direction may have been the Gyrojet Rocket Gun, designed in 1961 by MBA Associates of San Ramon, San Francisco.

Electrically-powered machine guns, capable of a rate of fire of up to 6000 rounds per minute, have been produced by the General Electric Company, of Burlington, Vermont, and are in service with United States forces. At present such weapons are mounted in vehicles and aircraft, but alterations in the design of ammunition may eventually lead to the production of electrically operated smallarms.

As a number of governments and private companies, with immense research facilities, are constantly trying to develop new firearms, new infantry weapons may become obsolescent within a very few years of their inception.

Revolver

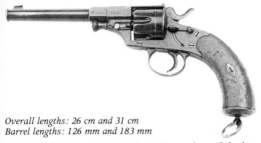

Overall lengths: 26 cm and 31 cm
Barrel lengths: 126 mm and 183 mm

The example shown is a typical service revolver of the last quarter of the nineteenth century. It is a German Army model 1879 revolver, made at Suhl in 1880. These were made by the government arsenal at Erfurt, and by various private firms, usually Schilling, Haenel or Sauer at Suhl, or Mauser at Oberndorf-am-Neckar. The design was approved by one of the various commissions choosing weapons for the German Army. It was obsolescent when chosen.

These are single action revolvers: the hammer has to be cocked before each shot. This type of revolver is held to be more accurate than the double action, as the aim is not distorted by the firer's having to raise the hammer with the trigger. A less conservative revolver of 1880 would have been capable of both single and double action. Loading is done through a port on the right side of the gun: the cylinder can be turned past the port when the hammer is at half-cock. To take out empty cases one has to remove the cylinder bodily by pulling its axle out from the front, and use the axle to poke the cases out of the cylinder. Alternatively one can rotate the cylinder past the loading port and poke the empty cases through it one by one from the front. Neither system is quick.

There are two models, a short-barrelled officers' pistol, and a longer-barrelled type for other ranks. The officers' model was introduced in 1883.

The revolver has six chambers, and takes 10.6 mm rimmed cartridges. This ammunition ceased to be produced in 1939.

PR

Hammerless Revolver

Overall lengths: 15–18 cm
Barrel lengths: 50–140 mm

Pocket pistols of the type illustrated were popular in Germany and Belgium during the first half of the twentieth century. The majority seem to have been made by Friedrich Pickert of Zella Mehlis.

The weapon is not truly hammerless: the hammer is encased in the high-backed frame. It is flat, and falls on a loose firing-pin seated in the frame. The object of encasing the hammer is presumably to stop it catching in the clothing.

Generally the cylinder has five chambers, but examples with seven chambers are found. Calibres vary from 5.5 mm to .38 in. The most popular calibre seems to have been .32 in.

Loading is through a hinged gate which can be seen on the right of the gun. For unloading, a ramrod is mounted below the barrel. This is pulled forward, swung to the right, and pushed back through each chamber to eject the cartridge case through the loading gate.

Examples with no trigger guards are found. Most seem to have safety catches, though since the pistols are double action only and cannot be cocked, it is difficult to understand how one could fire accidentally. Some examples have a trap in the butt to hold an extra five cartridges.

Gas-seal Revolver

Overall length: 22.9 cm
Barrel length: 110 mm

In appearance this revolver is typical of most military revolvers produced from the end of the nineteenth century onwards. This type was adopted by the Russian Army in 1895, and is known as the Nagant Revolver, after its Belgian designer, Léon Nagant. These pistols have been made at Liège, Belgium, and Tula, USSR.

The Nagant patent of 1894 is based on the idea that a revolver loses an important amount of gas between the exit of the chamber and the entrance of the barrel. To remedy this, when the pistol is cocked, the cylinder rides forward until the mouth of the aligned chamber encloses the end of the barrel. Special cartridges, of 7.62 mm, were also made. The bullet is entirely within the cartridge case, which is slightly constricted. The cartridge case itself enters the barrel of the revolver when the cylinder rides forward, so that when the pistol is fired no gas loss takes place.

There are two military models of this revolver, a single-action type, and a double-action type for officers. Various commercial revolvers of the same type were produced in Belgium at the end of the last century.

The gas-seal is obsolete, and was considered an expensive and unnecessary refinement. Unless a revolver is badly made no significant amount of gas seems to escape.   PR

Automatic Revolver

Overall length: 28 cm
Barrel length: 15.2 cm

This design was patented by G. V. Fosbery in 1896, and the majority of pistols of this type were produced by Webley & Scott, of Birmingham. It is known as the Webley-Fosbery Self-Cocking Revolver.

The principle upon which it operates is that the recoil of the first shot drives the barrel and cylinder back along the frame, cocking the hammer, and turning the cylinder by engaging the grooves upon it with a fixed stud on the frame. The barrel and cylinder unit were returned to the firing position by a spring.

A number of these pistols were used during the First World War. They were never officially accepted, but British Army officers were permitted to purchase any pistol which chambered the .455 revolver cartridge. The weapon was not suitable for military use, as a little dirt can jam the recoil action, which is more exposed than in an ordinary automatic pistol.

A few pistols of this type were made in .38 calibre, and some were made in the USA in .32 calibre. The type is now obsolete.

PR

Revolver

Overall lengths: 10.25–10.5 in.
Barrel length: 5 in.
Earlier .455 pistols
Overall lengths: 10.25–11.25 in.
Barrel lengths: 4–6 in.

This is a typical revolver of the second and third quarters of the present century, still in wide use. This example was introduced by Webley & Scott of Birmingham in 1942.

To load, the lever to the left of the hammer is pressed, to release the barrel and cylinder assembly, and allow it to tip forward on a hinge in front of the trigger guard. Ejection is by a component which springs backwards from the centre of the cylinder as it is tipped forward. These pistols are of .38 calibre and have six chambers. Conversion kits were available for training, consisting of a shorter cylinder for .22 ammunition, and a .22 barrel which fitted inside the existing barrel.

There are four basic military models, of 1932, 1938, 1942 and 1942/45. The first three were made at Enfield. The last pistol, illustrated, was in use in 1942 but not official until 1945.

This type of pistol was designed during 1926–27, and is a smaller version of the Webley .455 service revolvers of 1887–1915. After the First World War it was decided to produce a weapon less powerful than the .455, more effective in the hands of quickly trained recruits. Thus the .38 was adopted.

The 1938 model has no cocking piece on the hammer. These were for tank crews, who found that the hammer of a normal revolver catches on fittings inside tanks.

Automatic Pistol

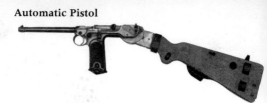

Overall length: 28 cm
Barrel length: 165 mm
Calibres: 7.65 mm, 7.63 mm

Hugo Borchardt's self-loading pistol, designed in 1893, was the first such weapon to attain any wide popularity. The design was improved upon by George Luger, and the Borchardt can be considered the ancestor of the Luger series of pistols. This is the first automatic pistol to employ the toggle action, devised by Hiram Maxim for machine guns in the 1880s. The principle of this is that the bolt is, as it were, a finger, jointed in three places. When it is in the flat position, the breech cannot open. When the gun is fired, the barrel and bolt recoil together, until lugs on the frame of the receiver guide the bolt into the flexed position. It then returns to chamber the next round. Loading is achieved by pulling the toggle of the bolt, in effect a knuckle joint, to withdraw the bolt head from the breech and allow it to take a cartridge from the magazine. The magazine is in the butt of the pistol: this is the earliest pistol to have the magazine so placed. The curious rounded receiver at the back of the pistol contains the recoil spring.

The Borchardt was always issued with a combined holster and shoulder-stock, and is reputed to be the most accurate of automatic pistols to be so equipped.

Toggle action weapons are now obsolete, as they require very precise machining and first class steels.

The Borchardt saw limited use during the First World War. It was not suitable for trench warfare, as the exposed sear on the left of the bolt enables the mechanism to be fouled by dirt.

PR

144

Automatic Pistol

Overall lengths: 6.75 in., 8 in., 6 in., 7 in., 7.75 in.
Barrel lengths: 4 in., 5 in., 3.5 in., 4.5 in., 4.65 in.

This was the first of John Moses Browning's automatic pistols to be produced at Fabrique Nationale, Herstal, Belgium. This was the result of experiments at the end of the last century, and was introduced in 1900. It was the first of a series of five Browning–FN pistols, which obtained wide military and police use throughout the world, so wide that Browning has become in several languages a common term for any automatic pistol. The other models were produced in 1903, 1910, 1922 and 1935. Some were legitimately made outside Belgium, the 1903 model by Husqvarna, Sweden, and the 1935 model by John Inglis, Toronto. Cheap Spanish and Chinese copies are found.

Some of the 1935 models have slotted butts to allow the use of a shoulder-stock.

The 1903 model is blowback operated. The others are recoil operated. Initially the recoil spring is in a tube above the barrel, but in the 1910 model it is fitted around the barrel, making the series even more streamlined.

The initial calibre was 7.65 mm, but the other models are usually in 9 mm. The 1910 and 1922 models were available in 7.65 mm. The first three models take seven cartridges: this was increased to nine in 1922, and thirteen in 1935.   PR

Automatic Pistol

Overall length: 8.5 in.
Barrel length: 5 in.

The Colt automatic pistol, of .45 calibre, is one of the world's most popular. Basically it is a Browning design of 1900, which first appeared in this calibre in 1905. It competed in the United States Government Trials of 1907, and was accepted for service in 1911. Minor alterations were made as a result of experience during the First World War, and the pistol as it is produced today was first put out in 1926.

These pistols have been made at a number of factories in the USA, in particular Colt, Remington, Springfield (the government armoury), Union Switch & Signal Co., Singer, and the Ithaca Gun Co. A few were produced in Canada at the end of the First World War: these are rare. The Argentine Ballester Molina, of HAFDASA, is quite a close copy of the Colt. A number of these Argentinian pistols were accepted by the British Army during the Second World War, largely for issue to underground units. The Spanish Llama pistols are also copies of the Colt, but are not normally found in the same calibre. The Mexican Obregon appears to be a Colt, but has more internal resemblance to an Austrian Roth–Steyr.

The Colt illustrated is an IRA conversion. A forward grip and skeleton shoulder-stock have been added. An extra magazine has been welded to the existing one, doubling capacity to fourteen shots. The mechanism has been altered to make it fully automatic, and then altered back to semi-automatic: perhaps the fully automatic version was found impossible to control. PR

Automatic Pistol

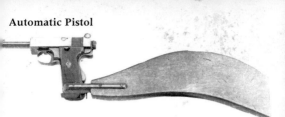

Overall length: 8.5 in.
Barrel length: 5 in.

This type of pistol by Webley & Scott, of Birmingham, was issued to the Royal Navy in 1915. It is known as the Webley & Scott Self-Loading Pistol. The first model, for the Navy, had a simple notch rear-sight, and no provision for a shoulder-stock.

The second type, of which the sealed patent specimen is illustrated, was proposed for the Royal Horse Artillery in 1915–16. It was not accepted. It differs from the naval model in having a rotating drum rear-sight graduated to 200 yards, and in having its butt slotted for a shoulder-stock.

A curious feature of this pistol is that it is possible partly to withdraw the magazine, locking it in place, so that operating the slide does not chamber the top round. In this way it is possible to hand-load and fire single shots, holding the magazine as a reserve until it is needed. This was a common provision on contemporary bolt-action rifles, on which a plate slides underneath the bolt as a magazine cut-out.

A special .455 calibre cartridge was produced for this pistol, which unfortunately also fitted the .455 service revolver but caused it to blow up.

Pistols of this type were put out commercially, in .38 calibre.   PR

Automatic Pistol

Overall length: 31 cm (1908 model, 22 cm)
Barrel length: 19 cm (1908 model, 10 cm)

This is the well-known German Army 9 mm artillery pistol, probably introduced in 1917, popularly known as the Artillery Luger. To produce it the barrel of the model 1908 was replaced with a longer barrel, a rear-sight graduated to 800 yards was added, and a detachable shoulder-stock was provided. The leather holster was strapped to this, and it hung behind the holster when not in use. These weapons did not differ otherwise from the 1908 pattern pistols, which continued to be made until 1941.

The example shown has the 32 round helical drum magazine patented by Tatarek and von Benkö in 1911, in place of the normal eight-round box-magazine. This made the pistol unwieldy. It was also used on the Bergmann sub-machine gun, whose development commenced in 1916. Attempts such as this, to turn a reliable pistol into an awkward semi-automatic carbine, tended to cease as the sub-machine gun and the assault rifle were developed.

The original 1908 model is the most popular and best known of Georg Luger's pistols. It derives ultimately from Hugo Borchardt's design in 1893, and was first produced by DWM of Berlin. At the beginning of the First World War production commenced at Erfurt. At the same time some were produced to accept shoulder-stocks, so carbine versions are found with the original short barrels.

In the 1920s a quantity of these pistols were made in England by Vickers–Armstrong, for the Dutch. A number were also made in Bern for the Swiss Army. PR

Volkspistole

Overall length: 28.5 cm
Barrel length: 13 cm

The pistol illustrated exists only in prototype. Apparently it was developed as part of a Primitive Weapons Programme of 1944, which was intended quickly and cheaply to arm the German Home Guard (*Volkssturm*) and other organizations intended to make a last ditch stand. This specimen is thought to have been made at the Mauser plant at Oberndorf. The delayed blowback action may have been designed by Viktor Barnitske of the Gustloff Works at Suhl, since it resembles his Volksgewehr Self-Loading Rifle, developed at the same time.

Part of the barrel of this pistol is rifled, part is smooth-bore. The smooth-bore extension to the barrel makes the barrel long enough for the delayed blowback action to work.

The basic construction of the pistol reminds one of the Walther P–38, the usual German Army pistol of the period. It utilizes the Walther P–38 magazine, which holds eight 9 mm rimless cartridges.   PR

Silent Pistol

Overall length: 36 cm

Clandestine forces, and individuals with clandestine duties, have sometimes been equipped with silenced weapons. These have usually been conventional weapons fitted with tubular extensions to their barrels.

An early effective silencer was patented in the United States by Hiram Maxim in 1908. Such silencers were used during the First World War by United States snipers, who used them with the snipers' version of the Springfield service rifle.

The example shown is a British Wellrod pistol of the Second World War. This is a .32 calibre bolt-action pistol, feeding from a rubber covered magazine which is also the grip. The bolt is operated by the large knurled knob at the rear. Silencing is obtained by a combination of two methods. The silencer tube contains a number of rubber baffles, and holes are bored in the barrel to tap off propellant gases into the expansion chamber in the rear part of the barrel casing.

The Wellrod is considered by many to be the most effective silent pistol ever made.

Baffle-type silencers are still widely used on sporting rifles. These enable game to be shot without startling other nearby game which has not yet been shot at. Many countries have stringent laws relating to silencers, especially when they are to be used with pistols, as criminals might find them useful.

PR

Knuckleduster Pistol

The multiple weapon illustrated was made at the Royal Small Arms Factory, Enfield Lock, during the Second World War. It may be the last such weapon to have been made, and is perhaps the only one to have been made in a government establishment.

This weapon is a 9 mm revolver, with knuckleduster and dagger. The knuckleduster normally acts as the butt of the pistol, but when a stud is pressed it is released to lie flat below the body of the pistol, so that the pistol lies in the palm of the hand, and the weapon can be used as a knuckleduster. The dagger also folds back beneath the cylinder of the pistol. The hammer is housed in the body of the pistol, and does not stick into the hand when the weapon is being used as a knuckleduster.

Pistols of this type were popular amongst the late nineteenth century Apachés (gangs of violent Parisian criminals). The best known makes are the Dolne and the Delhaixhe. These are six-shot, 7 mm pistols, taking pin-fire cartridges. Unlike the Enfield, they had no barrel, which, whilst it makes the weapon more accurate as a pistol, also interferes with the effective use of the dagger.   PR

Liberator Pistol

Overall length: 14.10 cm
Barrel length: 10.10 cm

A million of these pistols were made by the Guide Lamp Division of General Motors, Detroit, between June and August 1942, for distribution by the United States Office of Strategic Services to guerilla forces in enemy countries.

These pistols had to be quickly and cheaply made, of 'non-strategic' materials. The barrel is a simple steel tube, not rifled. The mechanism is die-cast, and the body is of sheet-steel stampings. The whole is held together by rivets, folds and welding.

To load the gun, the hammer is pulled back and turned. The breech-plate is raised, and a cartridge inserted into the chamber. The breech-plate is then lowered, and hammer turned back until the firing pin can pass through a hole in the breech-plate. The pistol can then be fired. The hammer is then pulled aside again, the breech-plate lifted, and the spent cartridge pushed out with a stick. The pistol was issued with ten .45 automatic pistol cartridges inside its butt. A sliding plate releases them.

Each pistol was issued in a damp-proof box with a sheet of graphic instructions.

The most effective use of this weapon was to enable the guerilla to obtain more efficient weapons from his enemy. PF

Rocket Pistol

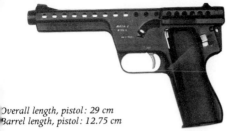

Overall length, pistol: 29 cm
Barrel length, pistol: 12.75 cm

This is a semi-automatic weapon with a calibre of 13 mm, known as the Gyrojet. It was designed in 1962 by MBA Associates of San Ramon, San Francisco.

The pistol is made from an aluminium alloy. The box magazine in the butt contains six cartridges. The barrel is grooved, but cannot be said to be rifled, as the grooves do not impart spin to the bullet. There are no moving parts other than the trigger and the feed arm. There is no recoil, and no cartridge case to be ejected. The weapon is intended to work under water.

The bullet is a micro-rocket 30 mm long. It is of steel, and hollow. It contains its own propellant, which is ignited by a percussion cap in the base, and burns through four peripheral vents canted at 20 degrees from the longitudinal axis of the bullet. The cant of the vents causes the bullet to rotate at 200 000 revolutions per minute. The propellant burns out in about 100 milliseconds, by which time the bullet has travelled about 15 metres. A carbine was designed on the same principles.

Some test firings show these guns to be inaccurate. There are too many forces acting upon the bullet, which cannot be too nicely calculated. The guns are comparatively cheap to make, but the bullets require a very high standard of machining and propellants.

To design a gun which utilizes self-consuming cartridge cases, or without cartridge cases, has long been a dream amongst arms designers. The Gyrojet guns may be the first of a new generation of arms.   PR

Shotgun

Overall length: 81–89 cm
Barrel length: 71–76 cm

This single shot 12 bore shotgun was designed by the Birmingham and London gunsmiths W W. Greener, and was made by the Birmingham Small Arms Company.

The action is basically that of the Martini-Henry rifle adopted by the British Army in 1871, designed by the Austrian Friedrich von Martini. Unlike the military weapon, it has a safety catch. This is incorporated in the indicator which shows whether or not the action is cocked. The lever can be seen on the right side of the action.

This is a general-purpose gun, which can be used for shot, or can fire a heavy rifled slug capable of killing deer or boar. These weapons also have a police use, either with buckshot or with the rifled slug, which is sufficiently powerful to smash the engine of a motor vehicle and bring it to a halt. For use with ball ammunition, a notch rear-sight is provided.

Martini-action shotguns have been produced in other calibres, but not commonly.

In recent years a number of military surplus Martini-Henry rifles, from Indian arsenals have been converted to 20 bore shotguns.

Terrorist Weapon

The weapon illustrated was made in Cyprus for EOKA. It is made from a motor-vehicle transmission column.

To load, the bolt-handle, which can be seen in the fired position, is pulled to the back of its slot, and pushed down into the vertical notch. The bolt, containing a firing pin, is thus compressed against a spiral spring in the butt-end of the pipe. The catch securing the barrel to the butt-end of the pipe is released, and the barrel is lowered on a hinge to reveal the breech. To fire the gun, the bolt handle is flicked up out of its notch. It is probable that 12 bore shotgun cartridges were used.

Even simpler 12 bore guns were made by Filipino guerillas during the Second World War. A length of pipe, in the end of which was a cartridge, was jerked into another pipe, which at its nether end contained a block of wood with a nail driven through it which served to fire the cartridge. The purpose of such weapons was to enable the user to capture something better.

155

Repeating Shotgun

Overall lengths: 85–115 cm
Barrel lengths: 46–71 cm

The repeating shotgun appeared in the la[st]
quarter of the nineteenth century, and attaine[d]
its greatest popularity in the United States. Th[e]
example shown is a 10 bore of 1887, made b[y]
the Winchester Repeating Arms Company [of]
New Haven, Connecticut. Weapons of th[is]
calibre were generally used by wildfowler[s,]
the majority of repeating shotguns being in 1[2]
bore.

The action is operated by depressing th[e]
lever which extends backward from th[e]
trigger guard. This opens the breech, throw[s]
out the empty cartridge case, cocks the strike[r,]
takes a new cartridge from the tubular ma[g]-
azine beneath the barrel, and lifts it into th[e]
breech. This class of gun has been largel[y]
superseded by recoil operated, gas operate[d]
and pump-action guns.

The repeating shotgun has always had [a]
police use, originally loaded with buckshot as [a]
guard or anti-riot weapon, and at presen[t]
loaded with CS gas cartridges as an anti-ri[ot]
weapon. It seems to have seen its first militar[y]
use with United States forces during the Fir[st]
World War. Loaded with buckshot, it was a[n]
effective weapon for slowing an assault on [a]
trench or arming sentries. Some militar[y]
weapons were provided with a bayonet lug.

A 12 bore assault shotgun is being built b[y]
WAK Incorporated of Medway, Ohio. It i[s]
capable of fully-automatic fire, and has a 2[0]
round drum magazine or a five round box. Th[e]
object is to provide the leading man in a[n]
infantry platoon with greater fire-power. Th[e]
weapon can fire any commercial ammuniti[on]
from small shot to rifled slugs.

Rifle

Overall lengths: 94.40–129.50 cm
Barrel lengths: 45.10–80 cm
Calibre: 8 mm
Magazines: 3 or 8 round tube

These rifles are named after Lieutenant Colonel Nicolas Lebel, a member of a commission set up by the French Army in 1884, which was charged with designing a rifle capable of using a metallic, smokeless powder, bottle-necked cartridge, designed by the chemist Vieille and Captain Desaleux.

The weapon was accepted for the French service in 1886, and was the first rifle accepted by a major power to use a modern type of cartridge.

The example illustrated is a carbine model of 1890. The tubular magazine employs a lifting mechanism to bring up a fresh round each time the bolt is withdrawn. This system was devised by the Austrian Kropatschek in the 1870s. The bolt action derives from that invented by Captain Basile Gras, and was used on the Gras rifle accepted by the French army in 1874. This was a single-shot, black-powder weapon, and was replaced by the Lebel. The Lebel rifle remained in service, with various modifications, until the Second World War.

PR

Rifle

Overall lengths: 102–127 cm
Barrel lengths: 53–76 cm

During the 1880s the British military authorities were studying various recently invented
magazine rifles, with the intention of adopting
one to replace the single-shot Martini–Henry
rifles in service since 1871.

The Lee–Metford was adopted in 1888. A
carbine model of 1894 is shown.

The bolt-action was designed by the
Scottish–American James Paris Lee, of Connecticut.

The most important aspect of these rifles i
the box magazine. This was the greatest o
Lee's inventions, and in various forms has been
widely used throughout the world. The cartridges are held by their heads, five at a time, in
a charger or clip. When the bolt is withdrawn
and the magazine cut-off pulled to the right
the edge of the charger is placed against
notches in the receiver, and the cartridge
pushed down out of the charger into the
magazine. The magazine cut-off enables the
magazine to be held as a reserve, and the rifl
used for firing single shots.

The barrel was designed by William Elli
Metford, to be able to tolerate the excessiv
fouling caused by the gunpowder in the earl
.303 cartridges used.

The Lee–Metford was replaced in servic
from 1895 by the Lee–Enfield. The barrel
were redesigned at Enfield, with more efficien
rifling for the smokeless powder cartridge
then introduced.   P

Rifle

Overall lengths: 127–133 cm
Barrel lengths: 76.50–83.20 cm
Calibres: Danish 8 mm, US .30, Norwegian
6.5 mm

The Krag–Jørgensen rifle was designed by Ole H. Krag and Erik Jørgensen at the Kongsberg Arsenal, Norway.

These rifles were first accepted for service in Denmark in 1889, and subsequently by the United States in 1892 and Norway in 1894.

The example shown was built at the Springfield Arsenal, Massachusetts, in 1898. This is an improved version patented by the inventors in 1893.

The most interesting feature of this weapon is the magazine, loaded through a trap opening to the right of the bolt. The trap is open on the example shown; it hinges downwards. On the earlier Danish rifles the trap hinges forwards. Five cartridges are loaded individually through the trap. On the face of the trap is a spring, which, when the trap is shut, pushes the cartridges round the bolt in such a way that the first cartridge to be loaded lies on the left of the bolt.

These rifles became obsolete in the American service when they adopted a Mauser rifle, known as the Springfield, in 1903. They remained in use in the Danish and Norwegian services until the Second World War.   PR

Bicycle Rifle

Overall lengths: 55–80 cm
Barrel lengths: 25–50 cm

This seems to have been an exclusively American type of weapon, popular during the period 1890–1910. The main manufacturers were Stevens and Wesson (Massachusetts) Marble (Michigan), and Quackenbush (New York).

Usually these were long-barrelled pistols, single shot equipped with a wooden or metal detachable shoulder-stock. These were introduced to be carried easily on a bicycle, in case strapped beneath the cross-bar. They were intended for hunting small game, or for target shooting: they are for amusement rather than serious use. Normal calibres were .22 .25, .30 and .32: others are encountered. Most used rim-fire ammunition.

The weapon illustrated is the 'Marble Game Getter'. It has two barrels, the upper being .22 rim-fire and the lower .4 centre-fire. This type has barrels which tip down to load others had sideways-swinging barrels. The hammer is hinged and can be locked to fire either barrel.

These guns have neither the convenience of the pistol nor the accuracy of the rifle, and are now obsolete, though pistols are still sometimes used for hunting small game in the USA.

Take-Down Rifle

Overall length: 118 cm (K98 k)
Barrel length: 60 cm (K98 k)

During the Second World War, a number of experiments were made with rifles that fold, or that unscrew into two pieces. These were intended for the use of paratroops.

The example illustrated is a German Kar 98 k rifle, built in 1942. When the lever on the left of the stock is lowered, as shown, the entire barrel and fore end stock of the rifle can be unscrewed from the breech. The Japanese also introduced a take-down rifle of the same type in the same year, based on their Arisaka Type 99 short rifle. In both cases the barrel is locked into the breech by an interrupted thread screw. The Germans seem not to have progressed with theirs, but the Japanese weapon went into service, and it was found that the barrels tended to work loose. A further type of barrel locking mechanism was introduced, in which a key is passed through the receiver and engages a slot in the barrel.

Further collapsible rifles were more easily and efficiently produced by hinging the stocks in the small of the butt. A large proportion of post-war assault rifles and sub-machine guns have hinged or telescoping butts.

English shotguns, generally of .410 calibre, are found, whose butts fold forward beneath their barrels. These were reputedly used by poachers and gamekeepers.   PR

Sporting Rifle

Overall length: 96.50 cm
Barrel length: 56 cm
Magazines: 8 and 16 round boxes

A typical modern sporting rifle is shown.
was made at Brno, Czechoslovakia.

This is a blowback-operated semi-automat
weapon. Loading is effected by releasing th
magazine, done by pressing the lever betwee
it and the trigger guard. The magazine is the
filled and returned. The bolt is pulled back b
the cocking handle and allowed to rid
forward, taking the first cartridge from th
magazine and driving it into the chamber. Th
gun is then fired, and the explosion push
back the bolt, throws out the empty cartridg
and returns to chamber the next cartridg
For a sporting rifle a relatively high rate of fir
can thus be maintained.

Two folding notch sights are graduated to
and 75 metres. These fold down in order not
interfere with the telescopic sight which
often used.

The ammunition is .22 Long Rifle, often
supersonic 'dum-dum' type bullet. The
weapons are not usually suitable for .22 sh
cartridges, used for vermin control, as the
cartridges develop insufficient pressure
drive back the bolt enough for the action
operate fully.

This weapon is similar in layout to th
7.92 mm army rifles designed by Josef
Frantisek Koucky, but those are gas operate

Survival Rifle

Overall length: assembled 89 cm, packed 43 cm
Barrel length: 40 cm

In the mid-1950s the United States Air Force became interested in obtaining a survival rifle. This was intended to enable aircrew who had parachuted or been obliged to land in enemy or isolated places, to obtain food, and if necessary to defend themselves. This rifle had to be a light, simple, and robust weapon. The Armalite Division of Fairchild Engine and Airplane Corporation, at Costa Mesa, California, were approached.

Armalite developed the weapon illustrated, the AR–5, and this, with minor modifications, was accepted by the United States Air Force, as the MA–1. The rifle is shown in its taken-down form. The action, magazine, barrel and butt, can be assembled or taken down rapidly. The working parts and barrel pack away neatly into the butt, and are protected from earth and water by the rubber butt pad. The butt is made of fibreglass, and the whole rifle floats.

A civilian form of the rifle, the AR–7 or Explorer, was put out in 1958, and apparently makes a good adventure training rifle. The AR–5 has a bolt action, and takes the .22 Hornet cartridge: a high velocity round. The AR–7 is less powerful and less rugged. It takes the normal .22 Long Rifle cartridge, and has a blowback action. It weighs $2\frac{3}{4}$ lb.   PR

Automatic Rifle

Overall length: 110.50 cm (Mexican model)
Barrel length: 57.70 cm (Mexican model)
*Magazines: 8 and 20 round boxes, 30 round
drums*
Calibres: 7 mm, 7.5 mm

This is a Mexican designed rifle of the 1890s,
patented in 1907 by the inventor, Manuel
Mondragon. It is named the Mondragon rifle
after him, and was one of the first automatic
rifles in military use.

There were inadequate facilities for the
manufacture of this rifle in Mexico, and the
inventor took it to the United States, where he
patented it but was unable to find a manufacturer. They were eventually made in Switzer-
land by the Swiss Industrial Company (SIG) at
Neuhausen. Like all SIG products of the
period, they were beautifully made of first
class materials.

The operation is basically that of a bolt
action rifle, but gas is tapped from the barrel to
drive a piston which returns the bolt to
continue fire. It is possible to disconnect the
gas system and use the rifle as a normal bolt-
action arm: military authorities of the time did
not trust gas operation.

At the beginning of the First World War the
Germans bought some of these rifles, many of
which they fitted with Tatarek & von Benkö
helical drum magazines, of which they
were fond. These magazines protrude from the
bottom of the rifle to such an extent as to make
firing from the prone position difficult. These
rifles, especially with the TvB magazines, were
too delicate to withstand the mud of the
trenches, and were not long in use. PR

Assault Rifle

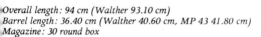

Overall length: 94 cm (Walther 93.10 cm)
Barrel length: 36.40 cm (Walther 40.60 cm, MP 43 41.80 cm)
Magazine: 30 round box

The example illustrated is the German machine-carbine produced by C. G. Haenel of Suhl in 1942, designed by Louis Schmeisser. A similar weapon was produced, in smaller quantities, by Carl Walther at Zella-Mehlis.

In the 1930s the Germans decided that they required a selective-fire rifle to replace their bolt-action rifles and sub-machine guns. A type of ammunition intermediate between the old-fashioned full-power rifle cartridge and the powerful pistol cartridge used in sub-machine guns was required. A cartridge which appears to be a shortened 7.92 mm rifle cartridge was introduced.

The Haenel and Walther assault rifles were designed to be made as simple as possible, using as few valuable raw materials as possible. Many of the parts are of pressed steel, welded and riveted together.

The fully developed Haenel rifle was the prototype for the 1943 machine-pistol. A curious variety of this is seen with a curved barrel extension and mirror sights, the purpose of which is unknown. It is generally said to be a device for shooting round corners, but may have been devised to enable firing trials to be carried out without using a conventional range.

These weapons had considerable influence upon post-war assault rifle design, in particular the Soviet Kalashnikov, probably the most popular and widely used weapon of the type.   PR

Automatic Rifle

Overall length: EM 1 91.40 cm, EM 2 88.90 cm
Barrel length: EM 1 62.20 cm, EM 2 62.30 cm

At the end of the Second World War it was decided that the
British Army required a self-loading rifle. Many major powers
had recently adopted one.

It was considered that the current range of rifle and light
machine gun ammunition, developed at the end of the
nineteenth century, was needlessly powerful, and that 900
metres was the maximum necessary effective range. Two new
types of ammunition were developed, of .270 and .276 (7 mm)
calibre. The former was found to be too light.

Two weapons were developed, the Enfield Models 1 and 2.
The EM 1 was designed by Stanley Thorpe, and was based
upon the German assault rifle of 1945. This weapon was never
fully developed. A prototype is shown. The EM 2 was
designed by Stephen Kenneth Janson, formerly a Polish
designer at Radom and Stalowa Wola.

Both weapons were of the bullpup design shown, since
accepted by many modern arms designers. Because the
magazine lies behind the trigger, the balance is excellent. The
design permits a different barrel length to overall length ratio,
giving a short, compact weapon with the accuracy of a bolt
action rifle and a considerably increased rate of fire.

Despite its good performance, the weapon was not adopted
as enormous supplies of conventional arms and ammunition
remained to be used up. There was opposition to using
ammunition of such a small calibre, and the 7.62 mm NATO
cartridge was adopted in 1957.

Weapons of this layout, in even smaller calibres, will
doubtless be adopted in future.

PM

Automatic Rifle

Overall length: 77 cm, LSW 90 cm
Barrel length: 51.85 cm, LSW 64.6 cm

It is now recognized that the 7.62 mm NATO cartridge adopted in the 1950s is more powerful than it needs to be. The majority of infantry engagements take place at less than 275 metres, so an effective maximum range of 900 metres is sufficient.

The NATO forces are seeking a new generation of smallarms, and the competing weapons will be evaluated in West Germany during 1977–1979. The weapon shown is a British entry, designed at the Royal Small Arms Factory, Enfield Lock. It is of 4.85 mm calibre, but if this should prove unacceptable, the weapon can be built in another calibre.

A Light Support Weapon of the same general appearance as the weapon illustrated has also been built, to replace the current general-purpose machine gun. The two guns have 80 per cent commonality of parts.

The personal weapon is more than 2 lb lighter than the current service rifle, and the ammunition is less than half the weight, allowing a greater quantity to be carried.

The bullpup design, resembling that of the EM 1 and EM 2, makes the weapon easier to handle in vehicles and other confined spaces, without sacrificing barrel length.

The magazine of the weapon illustrated is a twenty round box, and that of the Light Support Weapon a thirty round box. The two are interchangeable.   PR

Combined Rifle and Grenade-Launcher

Overall length, original rifle: 12.90 cm
Barrel length, original rifle: 78 cm

This 6.5 mm rifle for the Italian Army was developed at Turin in the early 1890s. It is a six round bolt-action weapon, known as the Mannlicher–Parravicino–Carcano. Apart from the magazine, the design has nothing to do with Ferdinand von Mannlicher. The bolt action is a Mauser design of 1889. General Parravicino was president of the rifle's selection committee, and Salvatore Carcano was the armourer who developed it.

The weapon shown is the 1924 model, made by cutting down the barrels of earlier models left from the First World War. The grenade-launcher on the right side of the gun was introduced in 1928. The same bolt is employed for the rifle as for the launcher, the trigger mechanism being interlinked. The bolt is taken out of the rifle and inserted into the receiver of the grenade-launcher.

At this time the majority of normal rifles could launch grenades with an adaptor fitted to the muzzle. Special grenade-launching blank cartridges were generally used. This system is still in use.

The weapon shown seems to be the ancestor of the current series of combined assault rifles and grenade-launchers, which are largely of American design.   PR

Sub-machine Gun

Overall length: 90.10 cm
Barrel length: 27.90 cm

This weapon was produced in small quantities for the Italian Army after the First World War, at Villar Perosa. It derives from the twin-barrelled, stockless Villar Perosa light machine-gun of 1915, and operates on the same retarded blowback system. It can probably be regarded as the ancestor of most modern sub-machine guns.

The two triggers allow selective fire, the rear trigger giving semi-automatic action, and the front trigger fully automatic action. The magazine holds twenty-five rounds.

The cocking handle is unusual, being a knurled tube around the receiver, which to load and cock the weapon has to be pulled back as far as the front trigger and pushed forward again. A slot in the bottom of it allows it to slide along the trigger housing. For this reason the rear-sight is awkwardly far forward, in front of the magazine.

The rifle-type wooden stock makes this weapon much easier to handle than the previous Villar Perosa, and it is this stock, as much as the mechanism of the weapon, which makes it recognizable as a sub-machine gun.

Like most modern sub-machine guns, this takes a 9 mm rimless pistol cartridge. PR

Sub-machine Gun

Overall lengths: 81.25–83.75 cm
Barrel length: 19.75 cm
Magazines: 32 round drum, 20, 24, 32 or 50
round box
Calibres: 9 mm, 7.63 mm, 7.65 mm, .45 and
possibly others

This is an early sub-machine gun, designed by Hugo Schmeisser and built by Theodor Bergmann of Suhl, Germany. It is commonly known as the Bergmann. Development commenced in 1916, and the gun was accepted for service in the German Army in 1918.

A second model was marketed commercially by Haenel of Suhl in 1928: this was widely used during the Spanish Civil War. Further development took place in Denmark to avoid the provisions of the Treaty of Versailles, resulting in a 1934 model. The last model, of 1935, became the standard sub-machine gun of the SS, who absorbed the entire wartime output.

This weapon was the first blowback sub-machine gun. It differs from most in having the cocking handle at the rear of the action. This is rotated and pulled back to cock the gun. The advantage of this, over the usual slot in the side of the receiver, is that neither dirt nor the firer's fingers can get caught in the action. The 1928 model has a selector mechanism, to permit single rounds to be fired. The 1935 or SS model has a second trigger behind the first. The first trigger allows semi-automatic fire. When it is fully pulled it pushes the second trigger, giving fully-automatic fire.

The first model was initially equipped with the Tatarek-von Benkö helical drum magazine, as shown in the illustration.

PR

Sub-machine Gun

Overall length: 85.75 cm
Barrel length: 26.60 cm
Magazines: 18, 20 or 30 round boxes, 50 or 100 round drums
Calibre: .45

This is the 1928 model of the Thompson sub-machine gun, widely known as the tommy-gun. The type was initially marketed in 1921, but none were accepted for military use until 1928. They were first used by the United States Marine Corps and by the United States Coast Guard. Their first combat use was in Nicaragua, but no quantity was produced until the Second World War. The Home Guard had a number, and some are still in use by American police forces.

Manufacturers were Colt (Connecticut) and Savage (New York). They are again being marketed by the Auto-Ordnance Corporation of New York.

The gun is loaded backwards. That is, the action is cocked before the magazine is put in, because the magazine slides from the right, and cannot pass the bolt when it is forward. The action is on the Blish system of delayed blowback. This depends on retarding the recoil of the bolt by the friction of slipping inclined faces. Blish units make for heavy guns, and are now obsolete. A selector allows automatic or semi-automatic fire. The type in current production is capable of semi-automatic fire only, and is intended for collectors.

A weapon of similar appearance is the 1935 Hyde, designed by George Hyde and made by Marlin (Connecticut). This has simple blowback action, and a Bergmann type cocking handle at the rear of the receiver. PR

171

Sub-machine Gun

Overall length: 85.10 cm
Barrel length: 19.60 cm
Magazine: 32 round box
Calibres: 7.63 mm, 7.65 mm, 9 mm

The Steyr–Solothurn is often regarded as a German weapon, and was in fact more extensively used in the German Army than in any other. Manufacture was commenced in 1930 by the Swiss firm Waffenfabrik Solothurn, then owned by RMM of Düsseldorf, and continued by the Austrian Weapons Factory (OWG) at Steyr: thus the name Steyr–Solothurn. Production ceased in 1940.

The gun remained in service with the German Army until 1945, and is still in limited use in a number of small countries, as it achieved a wide market in the 1930s.

This is perhaps the Rolls–Royce of sub-machine guns, being beautifully produced of first class materials, and much too expensive to have been maintained in production after the Second World War, when enormous quantities of surplus weapons became available.

The action is blowback, and derives ultimately from the Bergmann of 1918. It differs from the Bergmann in having the cocking handle on the right hand side, instead of at the back of the receiver. It is capable of single shots or automatic fire.

Long-barrelled examples are found. Some have bayonet lugs, Specimens were occasionally mounted on tripods.   PR

Overall length, stock extended: 63.50 cm (Uzi), 68.60 cm (M23)
Barrel length: 26.00 cm (Uzi), 28.20 cm (M23)
Magazines: 25, 32 and 40 round boxes (Uzi)
          24 and 40 round boxes (M23)

The current Uzi is used by West Germany, Israel, Iran and Venezuela. The manufacturers are Fabrique Nationale of Herstal, Belgium, and Israeli Metal Industries of Tel Aviv, Israel.

After the partition of Palestine in 1948, the Israelis developed an arms industry from the existing underground arsenals, which had supplied many of the weapons for use against the British and Palestinians. The Uzi was one of the first weapons produced.

The designer was Major Uziel Gal, after whom the weapon is named. The design derives from the Czechoslovak Models 23 to 26. The Model 23 was in 9 mm calibre, as is the Uzi, and was quickly replaced in the Czech Army by weapons chambered for the Soviet 7.62 mm cartridge. The Model 23 was dispersed, and a number reached the Middle East.

The compactness of these guns is achieved by deeply recessing the bolt so that it telescopes around the breech when in the fire position, to such an extent that the mass of the bolt is in front of the breech. Another space-saving and balance-improving step is to place the magazine inside the pistol grip.

The Czech weapon was the first successfully to use the recessed bolt system, common now.   PR

173

Silenced Sub-machine Gun

Overall length: 85.75 cm (65.50 cm folded)
Barrel length: 19.75 cm

The example shown is the Sterling–Patchett, in service with the British Army as the L34A1. It is made by the Sterling Armament Company at Dagenham, and was designed by George Patchett.

This gun is designed to replace the silenced Sten, which was one of the first sub-machine guns to be built with an integral silencer.

The intention is to provide a weapon capable of aimed single shots at ranges of between 50 and 100 metres, automatic-fire capability being only intended for emergency use. This weapon is virtually inaudible at these ranges. The sound which may be heard cannot be readily identified as gunfire. If the firer is in a well-concealed position, this makes it difficult for an enemy to locate him.

The original Sterling–Patchett, not silenced, appeared in 1943. Its successor is still in service with the British Army as the L2A3. The gun operates by simple blow-back action. Unusual features are rollers in the magazine in place of the usual platform follower, and ribs on the bolt which push out dirt through special vents.

Silencing is by baffles, and by rendering the bullet subsonic to eliminate the crack caused by its passing the sound barrier. This is done by tapping off the propellant gases through seventy-two small holes drilled into the rifling of the barrel.

The butt of the gun folds forward against the fore-end grip. The magazine takes thirty-four rounds. SA

Light Machine Gun

Overall length: 128 cm
Barrel length: 66.75 cm
Magazines: 47 or 97 round radial pans
Calibres: .303 British and .30 American

This is the well-known Lewis gun, used extensively during the First World War, and by the Home Guard and the Mercantile Marine during the Second World War. It was designed by Colonel Isaac Newton Lewis of Pennsylvania, and first appeared in 1911. The designs evolve from those of Samuel Maclean: the rear-lugged bolt may derive from that of the Swiss Schmidt rifle of 1889.

This was the first light machine gun used extensively in warfare, and is reputed to be the first to have been fired from an aircraft (in 1912).

Adopted by the Belgian Army in 1913, and by the British Army in 1915, it was well proven before the United States Army accepted it: they had refused it originally. The British form of the weapon, of which the first 1915 model is shown, was made by the Birmingham Small Arms Company.

The weapon is gas-operated and air-cooled. The expansion of gas at the muzzle pulls air through the aluminium fins of the cooling jacket from the rear. This cooling jacket was not used when the gun was mounted in aircraft.

The Lewis gun was appreciated because it was the first light machine gun available in quantity. It was rather heavy (26 lb), and its complexity led to a variety of malfunctions which would not have been tolerated later.

The wooden bird-scarer mounted on the cooling-jacket of the example illustrated is a contemporary training device, intended as a fire simulator.   PR

Light Machine Gun

Overall length: 53.20 cm
Barrel length: 31.75 cm

This is the famous Villar Perosa of 1915, sometimes known as
the Revelli, after its designer. It was made for the Italian Army
by Villar Perosa, by FIAT at Turin, and by the Canadian
General Electric Company at Toronto.

All these weapons have twin barrels and magazines. The
example shown is on the normal bipod mounting, for use as a
light machine gun, but examples with tripods and shields
were also made. Some were mounted on bicycles, and on
armoured vehicles, though they have not sufficient range for
this latter usage.

The gun has a retarded blowback action. The cocking
handle can be seen in the forward position, protruding from
its slot in the receiver. The twin magazines each hold twenty-
five rounds of rimless 9 mm pistol ammunition.

Because of its limited range it is not an effective light
machine gun. As it has a rather large bipod and no butt it is an
inconvenient sub-machine gun. It is awkward to carry, and is
relatively heavy: 14 lb 6 oz unloaded. After a few years of war
it came to be recognized as a conveniently mobile, quick-
firing, short-range weapon, and was used by infantry in
something of the way a sub-machine gun came to be used. It is
mechanically the ancestor of the sub-machine gun.   PR

176

Machine Gun

Overall length: 118 cm
Barrel length: 59.70 cm

This is the Vickers–Berthier, designed in France by Adolphe Berthier, and built in England by Vickers–Armstrong of Crayford from 1925. The illustration is of the second model, of 1929/30. It is a typical light machine gun of the 1918–39 period. The 1933 model was adopted by the Indian Army, who used it during the Second World War. A variant of it, mounted on vehicles and in aircraft, was used by the SAS.

The Indian version, built at Ishapore, is encountered as a medium machine gun, mounted on a heavy tripod.

To load, a full magazine is clipped into position, and the cover or cut-off pushed open. The cocking handle, seen in the forward position beneath the breech, is pulled to the rear, taking the bolt with it, then pushed forward, taking a cartridge from the magazine and chambering it. As the gun is fired, gas is tapped from the barrel. This pushes back a piston which returns the bolt, which ejects the empty cartridge case. As long as pressure is maintained on the trigger, and there are some cartridges in the magazine, firing will continue, in this case at a rate of 600 rounds per minute. This is a basic description of gas-operated systems.

The magazine is a thirty-round box. The curvature of it is made necessary by the steep taper of the British .303 cartridge, for which all these weapons except the French prototypes were chambered.   PR

177

Anti-Tank Rifle

Overall length: Mauser 168 cm, Marosczek 178 cm
Barrel length: Mauser 98.30 cm, Marosczek 120 cm

The appearance of the tank on the Western Front during the First World War caused Mauser to develop for the German Army the first anti-tank rifle. The example shown was produced in 1918.

Basically it is an enlarged Mauser rifle with a fixed bipod and a pistol grip. There is no magazine; it is a single shot weapon.

This weapon fired a 13 mm bullet with an armour-piercing steel core. Due to the powerful ammunition and the extended barrel, the bullet obtained a muzzle velocity of about 3000 feet per second, quite adequate to penetrate the tank armour of its day.

The Poles improved this design with their Marosczek rifle of 1935. This weighed only 19 lb 8 oz, against the Mauser's 39 lb. A muzzle brake reduced recoil, and there was a ten-round magazine loaded from five-round clips. The cartridge was oversized, with a 7.92 mm bullet. A muzzle velocity of about 4198 feet per second was obtained, but such a powerful round reduced the barrel life. After about 200 rounds, the muzzle velocity was reduced to about 3775 feet per second.

PR

Anti-Tank Rifle

Overall length: 1938 129.50 cm, 1939 158.10 cm
Barrel length: 1938 109.20 cm, 1939 108.60 cm

This is a German weapon of 1939, made by Rheinmetall–Borsig, Steyr–Daimler–Puch, and others.

The Mauser bolt-action was discarded, and a falling wedge breech-block used. In the model of 1938, the breech opens automatically after firing and ejects the cartridge case, as the barrel recoils into the stock. In the simplified model shown, the breech-block is operated by sliding the pistol grip along the receiver. The 1938 model gave a muzzle velocity of about 3975 feet per second, the 1939 model about 4150 feet per second. The 1938 model weighs 35 lb, the 1939 model 27 lb 4 oz.

The ammunition was a 7.92 mm bullet with a 13 mm cartridge case. Initially it contained an armour piercing steel core and a tear-gas capsule, which had no effect whatever and was not discovered until captured ammunition was examined. During the war against Poland, the Germans captured Polish ammunition of the same calibre, but with a tungsten carbide core. This gave better penetration, and was adopted.

As tank armour improved, these weapons became less useful, and were converted into grenade-launchers by the addition of a discharger-cup to the barrel. This can be seen in the illustration.

All anti-tank rifles became obsolete during the last war. The Russian Simonov and Degtyarev rifles were the last used weapons of this type. The place of these weapons has largely been taken by hand-held rocket-launchers.   PR

MISCELLANY

Since the flintlock period, gun mechanisms have been used to perform other functions than to fire bullets or shot. In the eighteenth century a number of gunsmiths produced flintlock tinder-lighters, and in this century a number of cigarette lighters have been made to resemble pistols. Whilst the collector may take an interest in one or other, or both of these extremes, both are too distant from the firearm proper to be considered in this book.

There are, however, a number of guns which are not what they seem, and which may confuse the collector or observer, but in which he may reasonably be interested. For different purposes, firearms have been made to fire a number of substances, from gas to rope.

A further group of pieces are not firearms at all, but are intended to simulate firearms. When these are made for military purposes, such as for drilling or for target practice, they may be of interest to those who have the guns which they were intended to resemble. They may confuse the observer, who sometimes cannot imagine for what purpose they were made: therefore some are illustrated.

Flare Pistol

Overall lengths: 20–35 cm
Barrel lengths: 8–30 cm
Calibres: 25 mm, 38 mm

Fire has been used for signalling since antiquity. Pistols intended solely to ignite coloured flares first appeared in the United States during the 1860s, and were used during the American Civil War. The earliest examples were percussion fired muzzle loaders. These were held upright while the flare burnt itself out in the barrel, and were only visible to those in line of sight.

The flare pistol as we know it was the invention of an American naval officer, Edward Very, in 1877. The cartridge fires the flare into the air, and it can thus be seen from a greater distance. This system won international popularity, and such pistols are still known as Very pistols.

The use of these pistols as offensive weapons has developed since the 1950s. Ammunition was made to enable them to fire wooden and then rubber bullets, to combat violent crowds. They were not accurate, but since they were merely firing a truncheon into a crowd, accuracy was not essential.

Some pistols were converted, by having extended barrels and shoulder stocks added. This enabled them to be fired with a greater degree of accuracy, perhaps at that portion of a crowd which might contain ringleaders. They were also used for firing CS gas. For these purposes they are being superseded by the anti-riot gun.

The pistol shown is German, from the First World War.

CMB

Fuse Pistol

Overall length: 18 cm
Barrel length: 9 cm

The type shown was approved for British Army use in 1881, and remained in use until the First World War.

It is not capable of firing a bullet. The intention was to provide certain ignition to the type of black gunpowder fuse then in use for demolition charges.

A catch on the right side of the frame releases the chamber, which folds over to the left. A specially designed short centre-fire blank .38 cartridge was used. An end of the fuse was inserted into the barrel. It is a single-action pistol: the hammer has to be cocked manually.

The barrel and frame are of brass. A clip, visible on the left side of the frame, is provided to enable the pistol to be carried on the belt.

QAB

Grenade-Launcher

Overall length: M79 73.50 cm
Barrel length: M79 35.50 cm

From the seventeenth century onwards persistent attempts
have been made to produce variants of normal firearms
capable of firing grenades further than they can be thrown.
This has generally been done by mounting a grenade holder
on the muzzle of the gun, or by placing a short-barrelled
launcher on the right hand side or below the barrel of the gun.

The weapon shown is a United States M.79 grenade-
launcher, of 40 mm calibre. It is a single shot weapon whose
barrel hinges downwards for loading. It is very similar to a
variety of anti-riot guns, of which the British version is the
Webley–Schermuly.

Some forty different types of ammunition are available for
this class of gun. In military use explosive grenades and
signalling or illuminating flares are the most usual. In training,
coloured smoke target-markers may be fired, and smoke puffs
to simulate artillery fire.

In police or counter-insurgency use the usual cartridges are
of CS gas or batons. The CS gas grenade can be effective up to
about 110 metres, but short range ammunition is made for use
in confined spaces. The firer has to be masked. The baton
round is a rubber or plastic bullet which evolved from the
wooden bullet formerly fired from signal pistols. The rubber
bullet weighed 5.25 oz, and its PVC successor 4.7 or 5 oz. The
PVC bullet can be fired with some degree of accuracy at
individual ring-leaders from up to 65 metres.　　　PR

Stun Gun

The curious device shown is one of several different types of modern United States household defence weapons. This one is the MBA Stun Gun.

This serves as a gun and a truncheon. The smooth-bore barrel is shown in the open position for loading. It takes a large-bore cartridge, resembling that of a signal pistol, but containing a small cloth pillow full of shot. This is designed to be non-lethal but startling.

The gun is held in both hands, perhaps with the knob of the truncheon handle against the shoulder for aiming, though a pillow of shot is not an accurate missile. The trigger, resembling the knob on a door bolt, can be seen in the illustration. This is operated by the thumb.

Some guns of this type have stocks.

Another type, designed by Mr W. R. Blake of the Tulsa Ordnance Company, is described as the Limited Lethality Weapon. It appears to be a .410 bolt action shot gun, with a new barrel of 43 mm diameter, and a tubular magazine beneath this. The weapon fires golf balls, propelling them with .410 blanks.   PR

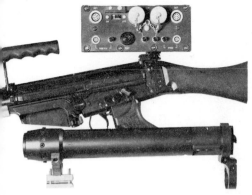

The equipment shown alongside a conventional military self-loading rifle is the Simgun, produced by the Solartron Electronic Group Ltd of Farnborough.

The Simgun is a short range, low-powered laser-projector, which can be fitted to a rifle or a machine gun. When blank cartridges are fired, laser pulses are transmitted from the weapon towards the target. The 'target' wears a set of detectors, placed on parts of his equipment, and when he is hit by the laser pulses, the detectors activate a device which gives off a puff of orange smoke.

Such devices have considerable training potential, since the soldier can fire his weapon exactly as if he were firing live ammunition, at live targets, in realistic situations. Likewise the targets can shoot back. The gallium–arsenide laser in use is completely safe against live targets.

The maximum range is 600 metres. Although this is considerably less than the range of the current generation of military weapons, it is greater than the range at which those weapons are generally used.   SEG

APPENDIX

The Expression of the Calibre of a Gun

The calibre or bore of a gun is the internal diameter of its barrel. This can normally be measured at the muzzle but in the case of shotguns, whose muzzles are choked the bore is measured at a point 9 in. from the breech.

The calibre of a weapon other than a shotgun is usually expressed in tenths of an inch or in millimetres depending on the nationality of the gun. Some common rifle and pistol calibres are compared below. However these measurements have become names for certain groups of guns and ammunition. The measurements are not exact, and are not always interchangeable. For instance, a type of rimfire cartridge known as .22 or 6 mm will fit most guns marked .22 or 6 mm. But ammunition known as .38 will generally not fit a gun marked 9 mm or vice versa, as the .38 cartridge is usually a rimmed revolver cartridge, and the 9 mm cartridge is rimless and designed for automatic pistols and sub-machine guns.

INCHES	MILLIMETRES
.177	4.5
.22	6
.25	6.35
.300	7.62, 7.63, 7.65
.303	7.7
.32	7.65
.38	9
.45	11.35

he inaccuracy of these conversions can be seen from
the entry for .300 calibre. 7.63 mm is the name of the
Mauser .30 pistol cartridge, whereas the Luger .30
pistol cartridge was known as 7.65 mm: quite a
different cartridge from the standard 7.65 mm or .32
pistol cartridge.

*To avoid confusion, such conversions should not
normally be made.* Both weapons and ammunition
should always be described as the manufacturers
originally described them.

The calibre or bore of a shotgun or musket is
expressed by the number of round balls weighing one
pound avoirdupois, one of which would fit the gun.
Thus, a 16 bore gun would, if it was not choked, fire a
round ball weighing an ounce. A 2 bore gun would fire
a ball weighing half a pound. This system of
measurement is imprecise, and upon modern British
guns the actual calibre, in tenths of an inch, taken nine
inches from the breech, is stamped as well as the
nominal bore.

A table showing some shotgun bores in tenths of an
inch is given below.

BORE	INCHES
8	.835–.860
10	.775–.793
12	.729–.740
16	.662–.669
18	.637
20	.615
24	.579
28	.550
32	.526

A shotgun, unless it is not choked, cannot fire a
round ball of its exact bore—it would probably blow

187

up. A musket seldom did fire a ball of its exact bor
The fouling caused by the black gunpowder wou.
have made it very difficult to load such a ball. It w
customary to fire a ball of less diameter than the barre
wrapped in a paper or some other material known as
patch. Without this, the propellant gases would hav
escaped around the ball as it passed up the barrel, wit
consequent loss of accuracy.

BIBLIOGRAPHY

rnold, R. (1958) *Automatic and Repeating Shotguns*, London

ailey, D. W. (1971) *British Military Longarms, 1715–1815*, ondon

ailey, D. W. (1972) *British Military Longarms, 1815–1865*, ondon

ailey, D. W. (1972) *Percussion Guns and Rifles*, London

lackmore, H. L. (1961) *British Military Firearms, 1650–1850*, ondon

hevenix Trench, C. (1972) *A History of Marksmanship*, ondon

ardner, R. E. (1963) *Small Arms Makers*, New York

reener, W. W. (1910) *The Gun and its Development*, London

ogg, I. & Weeks, J. (1973) *Military Smallarms of the Twentieth* entury, London

eterson, H. L. (1964) *Encyclopaedia of Firearms*, London

urdey, T. D. S. & Purdey, J. A. (1936) *The Shotgun*, London

ellers, F. M. & Smith, S. E. (1971) *American Percussion* evolvers, Ottawa

mith, W. H. B. & Smith, J. E. (1948) *The Book of Rifles*, New ork

ilkinson, F. (1965) *Small Arms*, London

ilkinson, F. (1968) *Flintlock Pistols*, London

ilson, R. K. & Hogg, I. V. (1975) *Textbook of Automatic* istols, London

inant, L. (1955) *Firearms Curiosa*, New York

INDEX

190